AIN'T
NOTHING
LIKE A *Real One*

Falling for an Inked God

2

D1316206

A NOVEL BY

TYA MARIE

CHAPTER 1

Follow Your Heart

Shacago

"You"—Deuce pointed to me then back to himself—"want to come back and work for me full time?"

I gave him a nonchalant shrug; I wasn't about to beg anybody to work for them no matter how bad I needed the money. The way my pride was set up, I had no problem working for Deuce until I found a replacement for Blue and then finding other ways to make easy money. I was Shacago, and I could think of a few niggas that would be more than willing to put me on. Deuce was only option number one out of respect for all he had done for me after I got out, but I knew people in higher places and wasn't afraid of calling on them to get what I want.

"If you don't want the extra help and I'm speaking out of turn, then I understand, Deuce," I said, holding up my hands appeasingly, trying to look humble when I honestly didn't give a fuck. "I figured with my brother being somewhat of a loose cannon, you might need some help taming him and moving high volumes of product."

"A loose cannon that you can barely control. Where is Xavier? It's been what, two days, and he still hasn't answered any of my phone calls. None of the girls downstairs have seen him either. So, Shacago, his brother's keeper: how can I expect you to keep watch of my product when you lost your little brother?"

"Deuce, you already know I ain't about to let anything happen to your product. I haven't seen Xavier either, but I'm sure it's with good reason. Trust me when I say I can get shit done with or without him, and you know that's the case or else I would've been dead after that fuck up with X's friend, Blue."

Deuce admired his manicured nails under the dim lighting of his office. "I could use your common sense and storage space in that shop of yours. With the Feds looking at me real hard, it wouldn't hurt to have you handling some business across town. I'll have everything set up for you by the end of the business day and ready to roll out tomorrow morning."

"I'll be waiting for your call," I said, shaking hands with Deuce and rising from my chair. "Good looking, Deuce."

"Not a problem," Deuce replied, inclining his head. "When you see your brother, tell him to call me."

"Got you," I said with a mock salute.

I exited the office and gone was my calm composure, replaced by unbridled anger. My hands were shaking as I called Xavier for what had to be the hundredth time. His phone was still going straight to voicemail, which I had filled up yesterday after he never called me back to help with the laundromat deal. This nigga wanted me to trust him with my wellbeing, but he couldn't act like an adult to save his life.

"Want a dance, sexy?" I was pushed into a chair and the next thing I knew, a fat ass was in my face, shaking and clapping like it was having a seizure. I was about to have one if shorty ain't get it out of my face. "What's wrong, sexy? You don't like my dancing?"

"Nothing personal, ma," I said, sliding out the chair without touching her, "but I ain't come here for a dance."

"So, then what are you doing in a strip club if you ain't looking for a dance?" she shot back to the empty chair. Her cheeks reddened when she saw me standing there looking at her like she was crazy. "Why you ain't tell me you got up? I'm over here looking stupid shaking my ass like I'm back in my bedroom practicing or something."

I had to hold back the laugh bubbling up in my chest. "You're new here, aren't you?"

Shorty lifted her head up and I immediately knew she had no business dancing in no strip club. Her large, doe eyes were wide and innocent, perfectly matching the pout her plump lips made. She was stacked in all the right places—with her DD breasts matching her slim waist and peach-shaped ass—but that had nothing to do with what drew me to her.

It was her skin.

"Has anybody ever told you that you have some beautiful skin?" I asked as the strobe lights flashed off her flawless, brown skin, giving it an ethereal glow.

Her shoulders sagged, and she looked like she was about to cry.

"You mean to tell me that I'm standing here with my titties and ass out, willing to give you a half-priced lap dance and all you care about is my skin? Are you one of them weird fetish niggas? 'Cause I mean, I don't really care, I can work with that."

For the second time since talking to her, I fought the urge to laugh. "I don't have any weird fetishes—I'm a tattoo artist and your skin is like the perfect canvas, that's all."

"Oh," she said, relief flashing across her face. "Good 'cause I really can't work with the idea of some nigga wanting to lick my skin and other freaky stuff like that."

"Nah, I'm just a canvas connoisseur by the name of Shacago." I held my hand out to her. "What's your name?"

"I'm Parai," she said and looked as if she instantly regretted it. "I wasn't supposed to tell you my real name. I'm Amoure."

"You must also be new," I noted. "What are you doing here?"

"I'm paying my way through college," Parai replied, staring around the club nervously. "Listen, I gotta go or else I'mma get in trouble again."

"Wait"—I pulled out my wallet and peeled off a couple hundreds and my card—"this is for the 'dance' you tried to give me. That's my card. Give me a call and I might be able to hook you up with a better job than this."

"You're not a pimp on the side, are you?"

I was about to reply when my phone started ringing. "Parai, I gotta take this call. Make sure you give me a call, aight?"

"Okay!" I heard her chirp as I rushed out of the club to make sure I could hear this nigga's lame ass excuse.

I picked up and went in on Xavier, not even caring to hear what sorry ass excuse he was about to hit me with. "Nigga, I have been calling you for the past two days, and you been ducking me and avoiding my phone calls! This nigga, Deuce, is coming for my head because you over here pulling disappearing acts, and I gotta answer for it! Now tell me where the fuck you are so we can pick up where we left off!"

"Sha-Shacago Stanfield?" the woman on the other end of the line sounded scared out of her mind. "I'm Dr. Darcy from Methodist Hospital and I was calling on behalf of your brother, Xavier Stanfield. He was admitted into the hospital two nights ago and has regained consciousness. You were the first person he wanted us to call."

"Thank you. I'll be right over," I said, hopping into my car and sinking into the seat. I hung up the phone and pounded my steering wheel. It was just like my brother to find himself in the middle of some bullshit. There were two things he couldn't seem to stay out of: trouble and panties.

******

The tag on the door had Xavier's name on it, but the person lying in the corresponding bed looked nothing like my brother. His eyes were swollen shut, and his right arm was slung in a cast. Black and blue bruises covered every inch of skin I could see, infuriating me more than X being off the grid for so long.

"X, who the fuck did this to you?" I hissed, keeping my voice down before I scared any more white people. "Nigga, don't even think

5

about lying to me about it either. You rarely go anywhere without your team, so where the fuck were they when this happened?"

"I'ont know, Shacago," Xavier rasped between his two busted lips. "Shit, can't you just be happy to see me?"

"Of course, I'm happy to see you, X. I wish it was under better circumstances, but I'm thankful that you're alive. I'mma have to call Moms and—"

"No," Xavier said, and for the first time in my life, I thought I heard him pleading. "Shacago, I don't want her seeing me like this. At least wait for some of the swelling to go down so I can look her in the eye and tell her that I'm just fine."

"But you ain't. What if something happens to you?"

"Can't nothing worse than this happen to me, Shacago. If the niggas that did this wanted me dead, then I'd be dead."

"How many were there? Where were you? Was it them niggas that robbed, Blue? I need to know so I can get a team together and ride the fuck out. Ain't no letting this go."

"I don't remember anything," Xavier replied. "I just remember stopping to get a Black & Mild from some store and next thing I know some niggas jumped me. I ain't get a good look at them."

"That's it? Just some bodega and a blunt? X, you gotta know something more than that."

"Actually, he doesn't," a new voice said from the doorway.

A slim, chocolate shorty wearing a lab coat entered the room with a clipboard. She was so damn fine I could feel a little cough developing.

Xavier let out a groan, and I knew all his ass had to do was smell her Marc Jacobs perfume and hear her brown sugar voice to know his doctor was fine. The way she flipped her long hair over her shoulder and gave me the eye told me she knew it, too.

"I'm Dr. White, your brother's new attending physician. We were understaffed in the clinic so Dr. Darcy was moved to assist with patients, however, I'm just as able to help get Xavier back on the right track."

Dr. Darcy was probably scared out of her ass about the black man that yelled at her through the phone, I thought, innocently scratching the back of my head. "Then I guess we have no complaints. How bad are Xavier's injuries?"

"Although they look really bad, other than his dislocated shoulder, your brother received lots of bumps and bruises. They're pretty superficial. His eyes will be fine once the swelling goes down and we've given him another MRI just to make sure there are no lasting side effects from the mild concussion he received. It appears to have made his memory a bit spotty."

"How long will he be in here for?" I asked, hoping that it wasn't more than a week because there was no way I could move all the weight I promised Deuce without some help. "A couple days, weeks—"

"We're still not sure; he's still under observation, Mr...."

"Stanfield, but you can call me Shacago," I said, holding my hand out. "I'm sorry for coming on so strong, but when it comes to my little brother, I just like to make sure he's good, know what I mean?"

Dr. White shook my hand and cracked a smile. "I totally

understand, Shacago. That's what I'm here for also—to make sure that he gets better."

Xavier groaned again. "Shacago, I know it's real soon to ask you this, but is it possible for me to stay with you and Zarielle, your fiancée?"

"Of course, you can," I replied easily, laughing at how this nigga was tryna block some harmless flirting. I could barely handle the love triangle I was in already, who said I was about to add a woman that could probably kill my ass without a trace to the mix? "How about I send Zarielle by to keep you company? Or Yandi, ya baby moms?"

"Y'all are cute," Dr. White said, shaking her head. "Anyway, I have to complete my rounds and check on the rest of my patients. I'll see you later, Xavier, and it was nice meeting you, Shacago."

"Bye, Dr. White," we chimed, watching the beauty walk out the door.

Xavier waited for the sound of the closing door to start with his BS. "Nigga, that's the future, Mrs. Xavier Stanfield. Stop blocking, you already got a bitch."

"And if you weren't half blind, you would've seen that she's already somebody's wife," I said, referring to the wedding bands I saw on her ring finger.

"So then why it took you so long to see them?"

"Her ass was in the way."

Rosé

I sat at the office table watching as Shacago flushed his potential down the drain. He was working hard at it too: his furrowed brows told me that whatever he was writing on that paper and double checking on his phone had to be accurate or else.

"You over there looking like Top Chef with the way you cooking them books," I said, peeking over and taking a look at the ledger Shacago was using to create the shop's finances. "I hope you at least plan on making a real one so that I can make sure the shop's finances are in order."

"Don't worry about that—I've got everything under control," Shacago replied, dropping his pen and admiring his handiwork. "Now look this over and tell me if it looks right."

"Shacago, I already don't condone what you're doing, so what makes you think I'm about to help you properly launder your money?" I asked incredulously. "With my brother, the last thing I need to do is have any parts in what you got going on over there."

"But if you help me do it correctly then you ain't gotta worry about your brother ever finding out about this. I already told you— this is temporary. By the time anybody even starts sniffing around this, there'll be nothing for them to see." When the expression on my face didn't change, he said, "Listen, if I even feel like shit isn't going according to plan, I'll make sure that the Feds know you and the team ain't have nothing to do with this."

"Could you at least do some tattoos to make me feel like this isn't a complete scam?" I asked, cocking my head to the side. "Do you really want the last thing for me to remember you by is a big ass gash on your girlfriend's side?"

"Funny that you mentioned that 'cause I found me a new model while I was down at Tasty talking to Deuce. She's still wet behind the ears and the most awkward stripper I ever met, but she's got this… quality. Wait until you see her skin, Rosé, it's like liquid silk. She promised to stop by today so I could show her some sketches and my portfolio."

"You mean me," I said, feeling slightly territorial. Shacago had tatted his fair share of women since we opened, but none of them had been hand selected. The last time he had done that was with me. "You want her to get a look at me…right?"

"You and some of the other stuff that I've been doing over the years," Shacago said casually, returning his attention to the ledger and after making sure his numbers were right, he snapped it shut. "You okay with that, right?"

"I'm fine," I said with a shrug of my shoulders. I pulled the ledger towards me and opened it to the first page. "Of course, I don't have a problem with you working on someone new."

"'Cause you do have a man and it might be inappropriate if I'm seen touching all over you," Shacago rationalized, studying my face and looking for the slightest hint of upset. "Seeing you naked and stuff."

I glanced up from the ledger. "We have a child together—I think it's safe to say you've seen me naked a time or two."

"Are you mad about me tatting someone else?" Shacago leaned in real close and grabbed my chin, forcing me to look him in the eye. "You're jealous."

"I'm not jealous."

"If you don't want me to tattoo 'ol girl then why don't you just say so instead of playing games?"

"Because you're the father of my child and that's just about how deep our relationship is. Like you said—I got a man. I can't police your talent. I don't have the right to do that," I finished lamely, lowering my gaze out of shame.

Shacago shook his head in amusement. "You're right—you ain't my woman and I don't owe you anything in that capacity, but as fellow artists in a partnership, I owe you my loyalty. You've been doing a good job at holding things down and there ain't another person in the world I would trust with my shop but you, Rosé. So I'mma ask you one more time. Is it okay if I tattoo Parai?"

"No!" I pouted, sitting back in my chair and sinking deep into it. "I don't want you sharing something so…personal with someone that you barely know. When you inked me, it was something special, and I don't want you sharing your evolution with everyone. I sound childish as fuck, don't I?"

"No, you sound real and I can respect your logic. Now I gotta figure out what to tell shorty when she shows up."

I was about to offer a suggestion when there was a knock on the door and in walked a gorgeous woman. The first thought that came to mind was a doll. Everything from her full lips to her pert nose were perfect, especially the luminous brown skin covering it. I could see why Shacago would instantly be drawn to her, because dressed in the cute, hot pink two-piece outfit she wore, I was too.

"I'm not interrupting anything, am I?" she asked nervously, staring at her perfect pedicure poking out the Louboutin sandals she wore.

I hopped up out of my seat and extended my hand. "Of course not. I'm Rosé, the general manager. Shacago told me all about you and he's right—you're gorgeous."

"Thank you, Rosé. I'm Parai. You're just as beautiful as you are in your picture out front."

Shacago was watching me with the "what are you up to?" look on his face as I helped Parai into her seat and shot her one of my friendly smiles. "Have you ever considered becoming a tattoo model?"

"I've given it some thought and it's a possibility, but I'm in school to become a lawyer and I think full body tats might not work in that environment. However, I came because I wanted to get a tattoo symbolic of this new journey in my life."

"Shacago mentioned that you were stripping. How's that going?"

"I got fired," Parai said with a wave of her hand. "I'll be good, though. Maybe McDonald's is hiring."

"Actually, we've been looking for a new receptionist and I think you'd be perfect."

Parai looked at Shacago. "Is that cool with you?"

"Whatever Rosé wants, she gets," Shacago said without taking his eyes off me.

If only that was true, I thought. Because if it was, I'd be adding one more piece of Shacago's vision to my body.

CHAPTER 2

We Are Family

Xavier

"*F*am, I really appreciate what you doing for me. Not everybody will take someone in for a month, family or not," I said, following Shacago upstairs to his apartment.

Shacago waved away my gratitude and countered it with, "Nigga, you would do the same for me. You ain't gotta leave after a month either—stay as long as you want to. Zarielle heard about what happened, and she's also concerned about you. You should've seen the worried look on her face when I told her what happened."

I bit my tongue so hard, I was almost positive that I drew blood. Zarielle's dumb ass should be worried because it was her cousin that did this to me. She better pray Shacago stayed in the house for the night or else I might beat her ass. I was still getting my strength up after being in the hospital for a week, but that didn't mean I wasn't above using the little bit I had left to teach a bitch a lesson.

"Well then, I'm sure she gon' be happy to see I'm good," I said, stepping into the house and dropping my bag on the floor at the sight in front of me.

Zarielle was sitting at the kitchen table serving Quan what looked to be lunch made for a king. Nigga had a big ass club sandwich set in front of him with a bowl overflowing with potato chips and a glass of ice cold Pepsi. Zarielle sashayed over to Shacago and wrapped her arms around him, giving him a passionate kiss on the lips like I wasn't even standing there.

"Baby, I didn't even know you were on your way back so fast. Lemme go and get your sandwiches ready. It's good to see you feeling better, Xavier," she said, giving me a small smile and hurrying into the kitchen.

"Make sure our sandwiches look just as good, bae," Shacago called out jokingly as he walked over to the table and held his hand out to Quan, who stood up to greet him like they were old buddies or something. "Zarielle did tell me that her cousin was gon' be in town for a minute. Wassup, you must be Daquan."

"Yeah, but you can call me Quan; all the homies do. You must be, Shacago, the fiancée she ain't stopped talking about since y'all met. Zarielle's momma been singing your praises to the whole family about how you've treated her better than any of the niggas she used to fuck with." This nigga was starting to get under my skin with all them subs he was talking with me sitting here. "She used to be with this one nigga like two years ago. The family never met him, but we all knew he wasn't any good because all she used to do was hide him. All that came to an end when he beat her face in with the butt of his gun. I was ready to kill that nigga, but he went ghost. Then she met you and started making her family proud again."

I wanted to tell this clown ass nigga that I ain't beat Zarielle with the butt of my gun—I used my hands like a real man should—but Shacago was looking like he was about to cry after hearing one of me and Zarielle's numerous breakup stories. He was about to pry when Zarielle entered the dining area with two sandwiches identical to Quan's.

"Baby, why you never told me about the abusive relationship you were in before we got together?" Shacago asked, pulling Zarielle into his lap.

Because it never ended.

"That part of my life is way in the past. I did a lot of building and growing so there's no need for me to even think about that pain," Zarielle said, kissing Shacago's forehead and squeezing him tight. "Don't you worry about all of that because you're the only man I'm worried about."

I picked up my sandwich and began tearing it up. Hospital food ain't as bad as jail food, but anything you eat after, tastes like a five-star meal. Quan was sitting there watching me as if he was waiting for me to start sweating or something, except he would be waiting a long ass time; I been pimping Zarielle out so long I'm numb to it. As long as she knows who her real daddy is, then I ain't got a damn thing to worry about. I spent the rest of our lunch listening to the trio talk while eating whatever was in front of me.

"Damn, I gotta make some moves," Shacago said, stealing a glance at his watch. "It was nice meeting you, Quan. If you in the need for any work just hit me up and we'll talk business."

"Most definitely," Quan replied as they dapped. "Plus, I heard you got a tattoo shop. I'mma be down there this week to get something done on my arm. We can talk some business then."

"That'll work." Shacago kissed Zarielle on the forehead and clapped me on the shoulder. "Love you, baby. See you later, X. Get some rest."

Zarielle and I sat there staring at Quan, who waited for the door to lock and for Shacago's receding footsteps before the innocent smile he wore became smug. I jumped out of my seat and pulled that skinny nigga over the table with one hand, sending plates and cups crashing to the floor.

"Xavier, put him down," Zarielle begged, nervously looking to the door as if she was afraid that Shacago would hear the commotion and come back.

My eyes bulged out of their sockets and I went to hit the nigga in his jaw when a sharp pain shot through my arm—I forgot all about my fucked-up arm socket. In a fit of rage, I dropped him and kicked the chair behind me, knocking it to the door with a resounding thud.

"Xavier, cut it the fuck out!" Zarielle shouted, helping Quan back into his chair. "Quan didn't come over here to fight. He came to—"

"To talk some business with you," Quan said with a shrug. "Since right now you need my silence, and I'm feeling real loud right now. So loud your neighbors might be able to hear me."

"Zarielle, get this nigga the fuck outta my face 'cause I ain't got shit to say to him!"

"Well, I got shit to say to you," Quan said calmly. "And to your brother, too. How you think he gon' feel when he finds out that his brother and pregnant fiancée have been smashing for three years? Shit is most likely to hurt, right, Zarielle?"

"Quan, we can work something out with you," Zarielle promised, holding her hands up and shooting him an appeasing smile. She gave me a warning look that said if I went against her this mess would be bigger than it already was. "Right, Xavier?"

I sat down in Shacago's vacant seat and stared long and hard at Quan before relenting. "What the fuck do you want from us?"

"I want $20,000 a month in hush money," Quan said easily. "That's enough to keep me and my boys living good while we staying in New York City. Might rent a nice lil' duplex in Manhattan and be on some Wall Street boss type of shit."

I cocked my head to the side and let out a bark of laughter. "You think I'm giving you $20,000 a month to keep your fucking mouth shut? It'd be cheaper to kill you and all them niggas that jumped me."

"You could do that...but then you run the risk of having y'all little secret come to light." Quan reached into his pocket and pulled out a blunt. Zarielle moved away ever so slightly as he lit it, the thick plumes of smoke obscuring his face. "I've given someone I trust with my life an envelope addressed to Shacago and if anything happens to me, then it'll be personally delivered to him. So, try that shit if you want to, bruh, and I promise I'll wreak havoc on your life even after mine is over."

Staring at this little leech, with his bug eyes looking like a fake ass Soulja Boy, I knew if I didn't pay him, all of my hard work and sacrifice would go to waste. "I'll give you $10,000 every two weeks. Right now, my money is tied up in some shit and I can't afford to give you everything in one lump sum."

"We can work with that. For now." He got up from his chair and held his hand out, the smirk on his face was enough for me to try and drop his ass again. "So, we got a deal?"

I had never been the type of nigga to bend or bow to any mufucka, but this was the price of slipping up and getting caught. I was forced to get in bed with a snake and figure out how to stick a knife in his back before this got out of hand. I shook Quan's hand and lied through my teeth like I did almost any other day.

"Yeah," I said, already plotting this nigga's demise, "we got a deal."

Rosé

I spun around in the mirror three times and turned to Cago, who was sitting on the bed watching me in awe. This was the third dress I tried on and no matter how much I asked for his honest opinion, Cago said he liked me in all of them. I was tempted to put on a trash bag to see if he'd still think I looked good. Knowing him, his high opinion of his momma would never change.

"Cago," I said, motioning to the mauve, latex dress I wore, hugging my hourglass shape and having my breasts sitting pretty. "Is this the one I should wear tonight?"

Cago gave me the thumbs up, which meant this had to be the one. "You look extra pretty in that one, Mama. Where are you going?"

"I'm going out with Auntie Yandi and some other friends," I said, not mentioning Marquise since it was too soon for Cago to know about any man that I was spending time with. "And you are going to bed because you have school tomorrow."

"Do I have to go?" Cago whined as he followed me to his bedroom.

"Yes, you do. You're going to go to school every single day and get good grades because Morehouse isn't taking anything less than the best. Ask your Uncle Eli—that's what he did and look at him: he's a successful FBI agent."

"Daddy's successful, too: did he go to college?"

I helped Cago into his bed and took my time fixing his blanket, trying to think of what to say next. I knew eventually Shacago would influence our child, but I wasn't expecting it to happen so fast. The last thing I wanted to do was lie to Cago about his father's education, but I didn't want my child growing up thinking that it was okay to skimp on his education. Being the bomb mom that I was, I found a middle ground.

"Your daddy didn't go to college, but he had to work twice as hard because of it. I know you're thinking that you don't need a college education to be successful, and while that's true in some cases, it doesn't work out that way for everyone. Your daddy wants you to go to college just as much as I do, okay?"

Cago scrunched up his face for a second and broke out into a smile. "Okay, Mama. Goodnight, I love you."

"I love you, too," I said, kissing him on his forehead. "Now which one of these books do you want me to read to you?"

Cago was knocked out cold when Yandi finally arrived. Eli took one look at our outfits and made us promise him that he wouldn't have to arrest anyone tonight. Once we gave him the okay, we were out the door, making plans for what we were about to get into and whatnot. To my surprise, there was a man dressed in an expensive suit standing outside of a Range Rover with the door open.

"Rosé, there's someone I want you to meet," Yandi said, grabbing my hand and pulling me into the luxury car. "This is my boyfriend, Quan."

I wanted to be impressed by Quan, but I wasn't. Everything about him—his Versace shades on even though it was eight o'clock at night, the ostentatious amount of jewelry he wore, and his loud ass gold and white Versace matching set paired with Balenciaga's—was just too much for me. Then I thought about Xavier's ass and realized they were two of a kind. My cousin obviously had a thing for over-the-top hustlers who most likely weren't shit. All I had to do was the same song and dance from when we were younger: be polite, make it through the night.

"Nice to meet you, Quan," I said, reaching over Yandi and holding my hand out.

Quan looked at my hand and stared straight ahead. "Nice to meet you, too. Driver, take us to Savannah's."

Yandi shot me a pleading look as I took my hand back and placed it on my lap. The rest of the ride was awkward, with Yandi turning up the music and trying her best to have her good mood bring Quan and me together. It only took for a nigga to act funny towards me once. When it came time to end the night, I planned on chucking Yandi the deuces and taking an Uber home. My phone buzzed and once I saw Marquise's name flash across the screen, I couldn't help the smile my face broke into.

Marquise: Hey, babe. Wyd?

He called me babe, I thought, blushing as I thought of something cute to reply with. *I settled with, Just thinking about you on my way to the club with my cousin.*

Marquise: Oh, really? What club?

Me: Savannah's.

Marquise: My boy, Lucky, owns that spot. I'll put your name on the list and have a spot reserved upstairs in the VIP section with a nice surprise.

Me: *How sweet of you. I'll be thinking of you all night long and wishing you were here with me...*

Marquise: *That's all I do every day. I can't escape you and I don't want to. I love drowning in you.*

I had to clench my legs shut to keep my pussy from throbbing; it had been a long time since my girl had any play, and if Marquise kept hitting me with all these sweet nothings, she was likely to pounce on him. Shaking away my horniness, I focused on my excitement.

"Marquise is so romantic," I gushed to Yandi. "He's setting us up in the VIP section at Savannah's."

Yandi's face lit up and she was about to reply when Quan cut her off with, "Me and my girl ain't sitting in no other nigga's VIP section. Fuck outta here."

"But, baby, it's Rosé's VIP section," Yandi said in her baby voice she used to get her way. "I wanna have some fun with my cousin that I haven't seen in like five years. You promised me fun tonight and after me and Rosé party our asses off, I can have my *real* fun."

I rolled my eyes so hard I thought I saw the "this fucking nigga" that ran through my mind. Yandi was my girl and I loved her to death, but she really had to do better with her choice in men because it felt like she was going from bad to worse.

"Fine. We'll chill up there for a little, and then we rolling out to another spot," Quan said still staring straight ahead.

"Thank you, baby," Yandi said, pecking him on the cheek and

cuddling up to him.

Since this pairing was more than likely to make me sick during some point of the night, I stared out the window and wished that I could be snuggled up with Marquise. The bright lights of Savannah's interrupted my thoughts, and before the car could reach a full stop, I had already flung the door open and stepped out. I stared to the heavens and watched as the driver scrambled out of his seat to extend his hand to Yandi, who had been told to wait before stepping out. Then came Quan followed by the guards he had.

"Who does this little nigga think he is?" I muttered, walking ahead of them to the bouncer. "Hi, I'm Rosé. Marquise put me on the list."

The bouncer opened the doors immediately, allowing us all into the club while everyone in the line started cussing. I heard him yelling at them as the club's music took over, allowing me to relax because I knew I was about to have a good time. When we arrived at the VIP section, I didn't even have to say my name because the bouncer knew me on sight.

"Ain't you, Rosé? That dude you tatted your name on was here yesterday and you got some skills. I was thinking about getting my mother's name on like my neck or something—you know what? We can talk about it later 'cause you and your people here to have a good time."

I danced my way into the VIP section, winding my hips to the Rihanna mix the DJ was spinning when a handsome brotha approached me. Had I not been a relationship and he wasn't wearing that wedding band, he would've definitely gotten to know me very well.

"Welcome to the new Savannah's, I'm Lucky Lewis, the owner and a friend of Marquise's. You must be the beautiful, Rosé, he's been posted up with all over Instagram. Tonight, I'm setting you up in my personal booth 'cause I gotta look out for my boy and his girl," Lucky said as I followed him through the packed dance floor to a booth with the best view on the party happening downstairs. "Your gift will be ready in a few, but for right now I'll send over some champagne. Enjoy yourselves and if you need anything, don't hesitate to ask."

"Somebody's got the juice," Yandi said jokingly as we got comfortable. "Look at you—ain't been here a month and you already pulling major connections. Next thing you know, you're gonna be charging for appearances."

I had to laugh out loud at that one. "Girl, ain't nobody coming to no club to see me."

"Why not? You're dating a famous boxing champion, your tattoos are all over the place, and you're gorgeous. Why wouldn't people pay to turn up with you?"

I didn't have to answer because a bottle girl came over with a bottle of Ace of Spades. "Compliments of Lucky."

"Because I'm me, that's why. I like to be real low-key and you know that, Yandi. Now stop worrying about my fake fame and let's turn UP!"

Once that bottle of champagne popped, it felt like Yandi and I were back to being young and wild. A reggae beat dropped and we were in the middle of the dance floor, shaking our asses like the retired dancehall queens we were. Our vibes must have been infectious because the DJ was shouting us out, causing other wallflowers to hit the floor and have a good time, too. I was cursing myself for wearing a latex dress, but I wasn't about to let it kill my vibe like Quan's salty ass was trying to. He didn't have a drop of champagne and spent the past hour watching Yandi and I have fun. My feet were killing me, but if sitting down meant I had to spend an extra second with his ass, I'd deal with the blisters tomorrow.

"Rosé, your surprise is ready for you," Lucky said, appearing out of thin air with glasses of champagne for Yandi and me. He'd been keeping us hydrated on the floor and I couldn't thank him enough.

Yandi wiggled her brows up and down. "Girl, hurry up and get it so I can see. I'll be waiting at the table with Quan."

"What kind of surprise is this?" I asked as Lucky and I made our way down a long hall and up a flight of stairs.

Lucky grinned at me before leading me through a door and walking away with a salute. "Something you're likely to enjoy for the rest of the night. Have fun."

Marquise stood there holding a bouquet of red roses, the smile on his face widening as I walked into his arms. I was about to start apologizing for how sweaty I was when he began kissing every part of my face—my forehead, my eyelids, my nose, and cheeks—until he planted a soft kiss on my lips.

"I thought you were in Cali working on an endorsement deal. I don't want you to miss anything because you're here with me. I know you've got so much on your plate right now—"

"It's hard to miss anything when you're the one that I'm missing," Marquise said, placing a finger on my lips to keep me from rambling on. "All that other stuff is for me to worry about. Your main focus is being here when I need you—like right now."

"How about we go downstairs and have a drink with Yandi and her boyfriend, then we go somewhere private where we can…catch up?"

"I'd love that."

I was expecting to come downstairs and introduce Yandi to Marquise, but all I found was an empty table. Lucky stopped by and told us that Yandi and Quan left as soon as he came back down.

"I know Xavier was a lot to handle with his childish antics and domineering attitude, but this guy is a diva," I told Marquise on the ride to his place. "There's also something about him that's…sinister."

Marquise took one hand off the steering wheel and rubbed small circles into my thigh. "Don't let no wack nigga get you all pent up; you'll have me sitting in the pen 'cause I took a jab at him. If you think he's not a good fit for her, then don't be afraid to talk about it with her. However, if she keeps picking the same kind of guy you might have to let her learn this lesson on her own."

"She should've learned it the first time." I intertwined our fingers. "I did."

"With your son's father?"

"Nah, with the guy before him. Tate was a demon and put me through hell, but Shacago taught me that not every thug is a menace. Without that love from him, I wouldn't be the whole woman that's able to open myself up to you."

I wasn't sure whether it was the champagne or the feeling of Marquise's hand firmly planted on my thigh, but I knew I had to have him at that moment. My lips placed kisses along his neck, each one ending with a gentle blow as I untangled our hands and used mine to stroke his throbbing dick through his pants. Marquise's free hand slid up my back and unzipped my dress, allowing the AC to cool me off. I shrugged out of my dress and mounted him, uncaring of traffic or anyone that might be watching.

"What you doing?" Marquise asked me as he slowed to a stop at a red light. "You tryna get us killed?"

I grabbed his face and pressed my lips against his, desperate for the taste of them. "I trust you to make sure we get home safe," I said against his lips as I ran my hands down his chest and unbuckled his pants, freeing his dick and stroking it as he fumbled around in his pocket until he pulled out a condom.

I slid down on his dick as he gunned it down the street. Every green light was a chance for me to find a new part of his body to devour and each red light was the opportunity for us to fuck each other's brains out. I was lost inside of his love, drowning in it once we hit his silk sheets. Unlike any other time in my life, I didn't want to be rescued.

CHAPTER 3

Ex Factor

Shacago

The stacks of money sat neatly rubber banded on the folding table. Of course, I had to give Deuce his cut, but at the rate I was going, I would be able to afford at least a down payment on a house in about another month. This had been the most fast paced two weeks of my life, and as much as I missed tatting, this fast money was easing some of the pressure I had been feeling since finding out that Zarielle was pregnant. She was already dropping hints about wanting a summer wedding, which meant that we'd be getting married before she started showing, so I knew I had to keep my hustling on 100. I was in the middle of bagging the money up for transport when there was a knock on the door.

"Parai, what are you doing down here?" I asked, peeking over her head to make sure no one was around.

Parai held up a cup of coffee. "I haven't seen you in a few hours, so I figured you might need something to drink. I noticed you've been looking a little tired lately."

"Thank you, I appreciate it," I said, accepting the coffee from her saluting her with the cup. "I don't mean to be rude or anything but—"

"I need to talk to you for one second," Parai replied, bobbing on her heels. "Just five seconds is all I need."

"I thought it was just one."

"No, I still need you to reply back."

"Fine," I said, opening the door wider to step out and talk to her. I barely had the door open an extra inch when she bum-rushed me and entered the basement. "Listen, ain't nobody supposed to be down here. You need to leave while I'm still feeling nice enough to let you keep your job."

Parai turned around and her eyes were lit up with excitement. "I appreciate the job you've given me, Shacago, but my tuition is expensive and I need something more. I asked the girls at the club about you and they said you get money. I'm not asking for a job too big, but something else just to pay my bills."

"I'll see what I can do—" I grabbed her by the arm but she was quick, shrugging out of my hold and taking a few steps towards the money.

"No, you won't. You're trying to tell me whatever you want so I can get out of here. Promise me a job, Shacago, and I swear I won't let you down."

"Fine," I relented, pinching the bridge of my nose and trying to figure out a simple job she couldn't mess up. "You'll handle a couple runs for me starting tomorrow. Make sure you're dressed casual—no bright colors or nothing. Lemme see how you handle that and we'll move from there."

"I promise you will not be disappointed. I know you're doing me a really big favor and this reflects on you, so I will make sure that all my p's and q's are in place. I will be running for my life—"

"Parai," I said, finding myself biting back more laughter. "I get it. Now stop talking about it so we can go upstairs."

Rosé was sitting at the front desk taking down a client's information when we arrived upstairs. She didn't say anything, but I could tell she had something on her mind and I would address it once we were alone. Parai took over the exchange, allowing my nosy baby momma to follow me down the hall to my office. Suede, who watched me go in both directions with a different woman, mouthed, "You the man."

"Why you out there looking at me like that?" I asked once the door was closed and I was far away from it—with business being slow this afternoon there was a good chance Suede could be listening.

Rosé took a seat on my rolling chair and began spinning herself around, her neon pink Huaraches a flash with each rotation. "I wasn't looking at you like anything, Shacago. You were the one who was looking like you got caught doing something you weren't supposed to be doing." She stopped at the perfect moment, our eyes locking. "Did you?"

"With who? Her?" I pointed to the door. "Why would you ask me some crazy shit like that?"

"I don't know…because it feels like there's something going between the two of you. Like there's this chemistry between the two of you that hasn't reached its full potential."

I cocked my head to the side and stared at Rosé like she was as crazy as she sounded. "Where are you coming up with this? After everything you and me just went through, you think I'm about to start something with another woman?"

"You noticed her skin—you didn't see the look on your face when you mentioned it," Rosé noted. "I did and it looked like—"

"Like what?"

"Like how you used to look at me when we first got together," Rosé said, and the smile she wore faltered long enough for me to see what she was doing. "I could be wrong, but I don't think I—"

"You are," I said, cutting over her and trying to ease any worries she had about me tossing what we once had aside. "Yeah, we looked like we just got finished doing something we weren't supposed to—I was setting her up with a chance to run for me so she can make some extra money. Ain't nothing but business going on between the two of us like it's always been, so you can relax all of that 'Shacago's got a side chick' noise before somebody hears it."

She didn't know I could see it, but Rosé let out a breath she was holding in and we began talking about regular stuff, like her latest tat and my plans to take Cago for the weekend. I was in the middle of writing down a list of things to buy for my place when the door opened and in walked Zarielle with—

"Quan, wassup," I said, rising out of my chair and dapping him. I planted a kiss on Zarielle's lips and grabbed her by the waist. "Baby, what are you doing here?"

"I had to show Quan where the shop was," Zarielle said, pecking me on the lips. She waved at Rosé. "Hey, Rosé. How are you doing? I haven't seen you since Atlantic City."

"I've been spending a lot of time with my boyfriend—Marquise. You remember him, right? Lightweight champion? Takes me shopping and buys me whatever I want. You should know because you watch all of his Snaps."

Zarielle cocked her head to the side and I could feel her vibrating with hidden anger. I shot Rosé a warning look and said, "Rosé, don't you have a client to get ready for?"

"You're right," Rosé said, wagging her finger at me. "There's money to be made because if there's one thing I can't stand is being a kept bitch. If you'll excuse me—"

"So, you gon' walk by and act like you don't know me?"

Everyone turned to Quan, who had been quiet for the entire exchange. Rosé squinted her eyes and leaned in a little. They widened in shock and her entire demeanor changed—her arms folded over her chest and the normally open Rosé became standoffish.

"Quan," she said, bobbing on her heels. "You look different without the sunglasses. Plus, I never got a good look at you outside of the dim lighting of the club. How's Yandi? I haven't heard from her since the two of you left the club without saying goodnight."

"I saw some East New York niggas I don't fuck with and we had to dip before shit got popping. You know how that goes," Quan replied, but I could tell that Rosé wasn't feeling his response. "I'll let her know you looking for her."

"Yandi?" I pointed at Quan in surprise. "This is the boyfriend Yandi's been telling Xavier about?"

Rosé gave me a curt nod and said to Quan, "Yeah, you do that. I'll see you later, Shacago."

"I guess you can't win everyone over," Quan said, rubbing the back of his head. "Yandi said Rosé and her ex were close, so I ain't even gon' sweat it…"

"Yeah, X is like a brother to her," I said, trying to continue the conversation when my mind was spinning.

Growing up in a family of law enforcement officers—from NYPD officers to FBI agents—when it came to reading people and getting a feel for them, Rosé was the best of the best. The fact that Quan made her leery made me second-guess handling any type of business with him. Zarielle was my woman and I trusted her judgment, but it was Rosé's gut instinct that kept me alive.

Rosé

"Why are you moping in here with a stank face?" Raven stood in the doorway of my station. "Marquise do something to upset you?"

I motioned for her to come in and closed the door behind her. "Marquise has been amazing—it's Zarielle's friend that's got me all pent up. That nigga is bad news and even though I can't prove it, I know he isn't going bring anything but trouble to Shacago and everyone in this shop."

"You mean her cousin?" Raven plopped down on my tattoo bed and laid back. "The only reason why I know is because he damn near broke his neck to make sure Parai knew they were related. He was all up in her 'assets,'" Raven finished with air quotes.

"He's supposed to be my cousin's boyfriend," I said, rolling my eyes at how unsurprising it is that Quan would be up in here tryna get some ass. "He spent all of last night ignoring me and then walked up in here like we cool. I swear on everything I own, know, and love that I love Yandi with all my heart, but she has got to do better when it comes to picking out her boyfriends."

"She better learn from her cuzzo and start going pro athlete shopping. 'Cause whether you know it or not, you're taking me with you to the birthday party for Vanguard's fine ass," Raven joked, referring to the rap superstar and best friend of Marquise.

"And come between what you and Kidd got going on? Nope, girl, you better stop playing games and lock that in already!"

Raven's cheeks reddened with embarrassment and she said casually, "I don't know what you're talking about, heffa."

I was about to tell her exactly what I was talking about when there was a frantic knock on the door. Parai came in and pressed her body against the door. "There's a woman here looking for you because you're fucking her man."

"Excuse me?" I said, getting on my feet at once.

Raven hopped off the bed and placed her hair in a ponytail. "Come again?"

"She came storming in here and said 'where's that bitch, Rosé, because she's been fucking my man. Tell her to get her ass out here and let her know it's getting beat on sight.'"

"Did she tell you who this man was?"

"Nope," Parai replied, popping her 'p.' "All she said was this has gone on for too long."

"WHERE THE FUCK THAT BITCH AT?!" I heard someone scream from the lobby.

Parai opened the door and I charged out like a bulldozer ready to knock this bitch on her ass. I had my fist cocked back when a familiar face jumped from behind the wall of the receptionist area and said, "Boo!"

"BITCH!" I screamed, pulling my best friend, Candice, into a hug. "What are you doing here?"

Candice broke the hug and hit me with a playful punch in the chest. "I came to fight your bitch ass for having time to be posted up all over the Internet with Marquise Meriwether, but not enough to call your best friend and see how she's doing. You got on the other side of the country and caught a case of amnesia, bitch."

"Damn, my blood over here pumping and y'all are hugging," Raven said, placing a hand on her chest.

"Candice, this is my girl, Raven. Raven, this is my best friend I've been telling you about," I said, continuing to make conversation.

We were all getting along and sharing laughs when Zarielle came storming out with Shacago hot on her heels. Quan followed behind, hands in his pockets as he watched to see what was about to go down.

"What the fuck is going on out here?" Zarielle barked with eyes for nobody but me. "Why is it that when I hear some loud ratchet shit, I know you have to be behind it? Were you part of this?" she continued, turning her attention to Parai, whose smile slipped at the arrival of this she-devil.

"Shacago's already told you about coming up in here tryna act like you run shit—"

"This is my man's shop, so therefore I do have a say in what goes on here."

"I didn't see you having shit to say when you couldn't even take the gun long enough to get anything more than a scratch!" I barked back, taking a step forward only to have Candice wrap a hand around my arm. "No, Candice, you ain't gotta worry about me putting a hand on this bitch because, as the general manager of this shop, she's gonna learn about how much weight I have to throw around."

"General manager?" Zarielle screeched. "Shacago, what the fuck is she talking about!"

"Zarielle," Shacago said through gritted teeth, "I made Rosé the general manager because I'm not able to be at the shop all the time due to my new business endeavors. Now please stop making a scene before clients walk in."

"Are you fucking serious?" Zarielle asked incredulously. "These bitches were just screaming at the top of their lungs play fighting and I'm the one that needs to calm down?"

"Bitch? I got your bitch, bitch!" I said, shrugging out of Candice's grip and getting within an inch of Zarielle before Shacago jumped in between us and started yelling for me to calm down. "I'm the one that's been calm. Shacago, you can forget about having my son for the weekend if it means that he's gonna be around this bitch. Y'all must have me confused with someone else."

"Bitch, please, you ain't keeping my man's son away from him, so you can keep it moving with that bullshit!" Zarielle shouted as Quan escorted her from the shop.

"Get the fuck off of me!" I yelled at Shacago, shoving him back far enough so he could get a good look at the words about to come out of my mouth. "Shacago, there ain't no need for that bitch to step foot in here, *especially* since she's pregnant!"

"The same way there's no need for you to get mad at Zarielle and tell me that I ain't getting my son!" Shacago shouted. "You can't withhold our child because you mad at my fiancée! So, I suggest you take today to cool off and we'll discuss this tomorrow when me and Zarielle come to pick up Cago."

I closed my eyes and listened as Shacago brushed past me. Only when I heard the door close did I open my eyes to find Raven, Parai, Candice, Suede, and Kidd standing there waiting for my reaction. I ran in place and rolled my neck two times to get all of my pent-up aggression out before I did something stupid.

"Damn," Candice said with a shrug of her shoulders. "I usually come in with a bang, but I ain't know it would almost involve a bitch's face. Y'all Brooklyn folks are different."

Xavier

"When you coming through so we can fuck?" Gabrielle, my girl over in the East asked as she pouted her lips. My dick twitched at the thought of her wrapping them juicy shits around my meat. I was so mesmerized by them that all I heard her say was, "…she always be with the bullshit."

"Huh?"

Gabi rolled her eyes and said, "I know your main bitch is keeping an eye on you after everything that happened, but I miss you and I want us to spend some time together."

"I'mma make my way over there to see you this Thursday," I said, recalling the day of the doctor's appointment Zarielle made the other day. "You gon' take care of daddy and daddy gon' take care of you."

"You mean we going shopping?" Gabi said, her eyes lighting up with excitement. A perfect day for Gabrielle is getting some of this long dick followed by shopping wherever she wanted. Unlike my seasoned bitch, Gabi's young—only eighteen—so a couple of Michael Kors bags and some Js was all she was looking for. "I love you, Zaddy."

I heard the locks on the front door turn and knew it time to cut this short. "Daddy loves you, too. I gotta go."

The front door burst open and in stormed Zarielle with Shacago hot on her ass. I felt heat rise in my chest at the sight of Quan following behind and calmly closing the door. Making sure I ended my FaceTime chat with Gabi, I set my phone on my chest and tuned into whatever was going on between Shacago and Zarielle, who had been doing good up until today. Zarielle was in a better mood since I was hitting her off with some good dick every day, but apparently, she needed to be full whenever she had to deal with Rosé.

"And who the fuck is that bitch that replaced Angelica? With all them titties and ass you look like you got her right out of a strip club!" Zarielle shouted, slamming her purse on the table.

Shacago scratched behind his ear and said, "I did get her out of a strip club, but Rosé is the one that hired her."

"So, we back around to the problem at hand—you need to check your baby mother. I don't care how you handle that bitch, but she needs to learn how to respect me!"

"You keep screaming that she needs to respect you when all you do is act like a fucking child, Zarielle! Stay in your fucking place and you wouldn't have this problem!"

Zarielle held her chest and stared at Shacago like he had three heads. "What fucking place is that?"

Shacago leaned in and enunciated every word: "Not—in—my—fucking—shop!"

"Fuck you, Shacago!" Zarielle shouted, pushing Shacago and storming down the hall.

Shacago followed her, his eyes set in determination to make sure he got the last word. "Yo, I'm not finished talking to you…"

With the show being over, I picked up my phone and started texting Blue, who was apparently having a good time down in

Baltimore. The nigga said they was treating him like a king down there and he wasn't even sure if he was coming back to New York anytime soon. I was staring at my screen, waiting for him to reply when I heard a cough.

"You need some water, fam?" I asked Quan without looking up from my phone.

Quan chuckled. "Real funny. I don't need no water, but I do need a favor."

"Listen, I gave you your money. I'm not about to be doing no favors for you so don't even think about asking me no funny shit."

"You either do me this favor or I walk in that room and give Shacago and Zarielle something else to argue about."

This shit was getting old real fast and I was gon' have to figure out how to get rid of this nigga sooner rather than later. "What you want?" I asked, giving up on avoiding eye contact and staring this nigga in the eye to show him that he might have the upper hand for now, but that wouldn't be the case for long. "Nigga, speak while they arguing and can't hear shit."

"You gon' be out for another week or two, so I need you to put in a word with Shacago, giving me your spot until you're ready to come back to work."

"I hate to ruin your little dreams of running Brooklyn, but I'm starting work this weekend. If you wanna tag along with him for tomorrow, then be my guest. I'm coming back strong on Saturday night, so all that shit is dead."

Quan shrugged. "I ain't too picky about the position—I just

wanna be on the team. I'm not even about to ask you if it's something you can do 'cause I know you can. Just hit me with the information I need for tomorrow."

Like any confident lil' mufucka, Quan had the nerve to walk to the door slow and steady. I reached between the couch cushions and wrapped my hand around my .9. The temptation to blow his brains out of his head was too strong. Three shots could end all my problems— he'd be dead and I'd be back to running my life. Then I thought about that letter he had hidden somewhere and knew even if I killed his ass, there was a good chance Shacago might find out shit he ain't have no business knowing. I pulled my hand out the cushion and gave Quan a mock salute. He was riding high right now, but once I got my hand on that person and letter Quan would be riding straight to a pine box with his name on it.

CHAPTER 4

PYT

Rosé

"I'm taking it that your master plan to come back to New York, get Shacago, and live happily ever after wasn't successful," Candice noted over her third martini. "He's got a pregnant fiancée and from the looks of it, that bitch ain't going nowhere."

"She has this hold over him that I'll never be able to break," I said, trying to explain Zarielle's reason for still being around without giving away too much of Shacago's business. "He claims that it's because she's a ride-or-die, but I think it's a fear of me running out on him again."

Candice finished off her martini and signaled for the bartender to bring over another round. I popped another boneless BBQ wing in my mouth and washed down the last of my drink. We had been sitting at the bar for the past three hours playing catch-up, which felt more like me spilling all my tea while Candice listened and gave her two cents whenever she could.

"You know what this sounds like? A whole bunch of shit you don't need in your life. I've known you for going on seven years and I have never seen you caught up in no drama like this, Rosé. Honey, you need to just focus on co-parenting and having some fun with that filthy rich boyfriend of yours. Life's too short for baby mama drama."

The bartender arrived with our drinks, giving me a chance to mull over what I was about to say next. "That's what I've been doing, but sometimes I feel like I'd take all of that drama just to give us a fair try." I felt much better when I said it aloud, and my shoulders sagged with relief. "Do you know how long I've been holding that in? It feels good to get it off my chest."

"Okay, so what are you gonna do about it?" Candice asked, cocking an eyebrow. "Are you going to figure out a way to break up this relationship and take a chance with Shacago, which means accepting that you'll now be in Zarielle's place and deal with her as a bitter baby momma for the rest of your relationship, or start something new with an emotionally available man who can give you everything you've been praying for."

"When you put it like that..."

"Yeah, you can feel the pressure and headache disappearing. Imagine dealing with what happened in that shop for the next eighteen years? We'd be sharing a cell in prison 'cause you know I'm helping you hide the body."

We toasted and tossed our drinks back. I did a small shimmy and said, "Enough about me and all my drama. Bitch, what are you doing in New York?"

"I quit my job and moved here!" Candice replied with jazz hands. My jaw dropped and I was at a loss for words. She dropped her hands and gave me a playful shove. "Girl, I missed you and Cago. That house was so big and quiet—I started going crazy being there all by myself."

"I thought you were gonna have parties and let your boo move in with you."

Candice rolled her eyes so hard I thought they might get stuck up in her head. When they finally returned, she cocked her head to the side and said, "Lemme tell you this. I moved Tyrese's bum ass in and you know on the second day of us living together this nigga had the audacity to have not one, but two bitches in my $5,000 bed on my raw silk sheets feeding him strawberries? Some bitches lost inches that day and that trifling ass nigga would've too had he not been so damn fast. How you leave your hoes behind?"

"Because he ain't give a fuck about them," I interjected, knowing it was only a matter of time before Tyrese got caught up in some shit he couldn't explain himself out of.

"Yeah, well that wasn't a comforting thought because all it did was show me that he don't give a fuck about me either," Candice said with a nonchalant shrug, but I could tell that Tyrese had hurt her. "I was in Cali all alone with no one to talk to—you know my family stopped fucking with me when I started stripping. So, I decided to come to my real family and look into starting over."

"At least you won't be alone on that journey," I said, playing with my olive. "Have you got a place yet?"

"Well, I'm renting out my house in Cali to pay a mortgage here, and I'm looking to buy a condo for at least $400,000. I haven't touched that inheritance money Winston, my old sugar daddy, left me, which leaves me a lot of wiggle room when it comes to pricing," Candice said casually like she was talking about some chump change.

I grabbed her hand. "I know it's not much, but I have $100,000 set aside for housing that I could put in with you. We could get a real nice place with half a million and I can start paying you back from now because business is booming."

"Are you saying that we're gonna be roomies again?" Candice said, wiggling her eyebrows.

"Back to the turn up we go," I said, screaming and hugging my girl.

It was good to have some of that California loving back and if there was one thing I could say about Candice is that she keeps things interesting.

******

"DADDYYYYY!" Cago squealed, running into Shacago's arms and wrapping his arms around his neck. "I missed you."

"I missed you too, little man," Shacago said, kissing Cago on the forehead. "We gon' have a lot of fun this weekend with Uncle Xavier and Little X. You like basketball, right?"

Cago nodded excitedly. "It's my favorite."

"Well then you should check out the surprise I got you in your new room here. Make a left and go all the way down the hall."

Cago wiggled out of Shacago's arms and disappeared around the corner. Shacago stepped aside so I could enter, those dark eyes of his taking in the form fitting maxi dress I had on. When I caught him staring at my ass, he tried to act all innocent like he didn't know any better. I shot him a warning look, knowing that the last thing I wanted to do was start some shit in his house.

"Somebody's in a good mood. Hot date tonight?"

"Nah, Candice and I were out apartment hunting today and I think we found a spot. This nice three-bedroom condominium not too far from the shop. It's a little out of our price range, but Eli's lending me the extra money to put in."

"How much you need?" Shacago asked, inviting me to take a seat at the kitchen island.

"About $30,000, but like I said, Elijah is putting in—"

"I'll bring it to you when I drop Cago off on Sunday," Shacago said resolutely. "Let your brother know that it's been handled. Don't even try to argue with me, Rosé. I've missed a lot of my son's life, meaning that I got a lot of catching up to do. I ain't about to have another man paying his way when I'm fully capable of helping out."

I was about to put up an argument explaining that Elijah would question where he got the money on such short notice, but the determined look in Shacago's eyes told me there was no point in arguing with him. "Fine, I'll let him know. I also wanted to talk to you about yesterday—"

"Zarielle and I had a long talk, and after explaining to her that you're in charge of the shop, it's best that she doesn't come there anymore. It'll keep the peace between all of us and keep the shop from gaining a bad reputation."

"I really appreciate that," I said, placing my hands on my chest to show my gratitude, "but that's not the only thing that I needed to talk to you about. I know Quan is Zarielle's cousin so that makes him your people, but something's not right about him. I'm not tryna tell you how to run your business or anything, I'm just tryna say that I think it's best if you keep him in associate territory until you get to know him better. I hope I'm not overstepping my boundaries or anything—"

"Nah, I appreciate you coming to me and letting me know what's on your mind. You've always been a real good judge of character so I value your opinion. I'm not sure who that lil' nigga running with, but he seems to be doing well for himself. If anything, I'll play it by ear."

Cago came running back to the kitchen with Xavier in tow, holding him by his good hand being that his other one was in a sling. I hopped off my chair and stalked over to Xavier, slapping him on his good arm. Cago ran to his father, where they both watched us silently.

"Boy, what happened to your face?" I said, examining the fading black eyes that were starting to turn an ugly shade of yellow. "Whose boyfriend did you piss off?"

Xavier's eyes widened momentarily and then went blank. He shrugged me off and took a seat on the couch. "I ain't piss nobody off. I got jumped by some pussy ass niggas for being in their territory."

"You going back, right?" Xavier had never been one to back down from a fight, but he was playing it real cool. "Right, Xavier?"

"I plan on handling it when my arm ain't in a sling and I have all my niggas ready to ride out. Trust me when I say heads are rolling over this shit," Xavier replied, his face turning to stone as he whipped out his phone and began texting.

"Bye, Mommy," Cago said, giving me a hug and kiss on the cheek then curling up with Xavier. "Love you."

"Love you, too, baby," I replied, glad to see how close he was growing to the male role models in his life.

"I been tryna to get him to tell me what happened since he woke up in the hospital looking half dead, but he wouldn't tell me anything," Shacago said as he walked me to my car. "What he told you back there contradicts what he told me. He claimed he ain't know who did it, but apparently, he does and he's hiding it. Why, is the question?"

"You're right. X ain't one to hide or be scared of nobody. He wasn't even scared of taking a whipping from Deuce's men. Who put that much fear into his heart that he won't speak up?"

"I'll find out soon enough 'cause me and my brother don't keep shit from each other." We arrived at Candice's Audi A30 that she had shipped here (I was really starting to enjoy having my girl on the East Coast). "This you?"

"This is Candice's, and as long as I fill it up with gas, I can use it, too," I said, opening the door and climbing halfway in. "Why are you looking at me like that?"

Shacago closed the distance between us, his lips nearly brushing mines. "I always imagined that when we had a child you would live like a queen. It might not show, but not being able to give you the world is breaking my heart. All I need you to do is bear with me for another month and—"

"You really don't get it, do you?" I said, cocking an eyebrow. "I don't give a fuck about having a nice ass car, house, or fancy engagement rings. All I've cared about since the day I met you is this bond, the same goal we share. If the price to have a car is blood, then I don't want it. Remember: we fell in love with each other's hustle, not each other's pockets."

Shacago looked ready to lean in and give me some of what I had been dying for since I came back to town. As much as I wanted to lean in and accept his kiss, I knew that no good would come of it because no matter how much passion we shared at the end of the day, he still had a pregnant fiancée. I leaned back and did what any woman with self-respect would do—slipped into my car and played it cool despite my heart hammering against my chest. We locked eyes and I inclined my head. Shacago shook his head, smiling as something satisfying shined in his eyes.

Respect.

Shacago

Zarielle was sitting at the kitchen island when I came upstairs, tapping her foot while staring at me with this smirk on her face. I made sure Cago was still playing with Xavier before I sat down to see what petty bullshit Zarielle was about to start.

"I saw you walk your baby mother to her car," Zarielle said casually. "Y'all looked real close and comfy until she shut ya ass down."

I placed my face into my hands and tried to control the anger I was feeling because the last thing I wanted was for my son to see me acting a damn fool on his first weekend here. "Is there a point to this conversation, Zarielle? Or are you just talking out your ass because I banned you from the shop?"

"You can't ban me from a muthafuckin' place I don't wanna be. As far as I'm concerned, since my best friend was murdered and doesn't work there anymore, I don't have a reason to show up at your bitch ass shop. You know what that means? Since your baby mother doesn't pay rent or contribute to this house then she needn't sit in my chairs and breathe my air."

"You really feeling yourself," I said with a grin. "Let's see how much you feel yourself when you're sleeping in this apartment by your damn self. Me, Cago, and X can spend the weekend at my Mom's house, giving you all the alone time you need since you still wanna be mad about shit you started."

"Well, you ain't do a good job at finishing it because you and your baby mother are catching up like chums while I'm the one with the short end of the stick."

"That's what you gave yourself acting like a damn child."

"If that's how you feel, then you and your child can leave and get the fuck outta my face. How about that?"

My phone lit up with a message from Parai asking me to meet her at her place. Most likely it was to pick up the cash from her drops. "X, can you do me a favor and take Cago over to Moms' house? I gotta handle some business."

"Got you, bro," Xavier replied.

I took one last look at Zarielle before walking out the door and wondered if sharing a child was enough to share the rest of your life with a person. At this point, the rest of the night was already feeling like too much.

******

"I hope I wasn't interrupting anything," Parai said as I stepped into her apartment. "I know what you're thinking—I like the color lavender a lot."

Everything—the walls, couch pillows, her area rug, and duvet—were an identical shade of lavender. The air even smelled like lavender. "I mean against the white furniture, it's pretty dope. Shit, I was mad as hell until I stepped up in here."

"That could be because of my Feng Shui. I've got everything in my apartment laid out right to promote positive energy and relaxation. Then I've got my lavender and vanilla aroma candles burning to create a warm feeling," Parai replied, motioning for me to take a seat on the couch while she went to the kitchen and made two tall mugs of tea. "Would you like to talk about what's got you upset?"

I accepted the mug of tea from her and took a gulp. "Damn, this shit hit the spot. What kind of tea of this?"

"Honey and chamomile with a couple shots of Honey Jack Daniels. You looked like you could use it to take the edge off. Now tell me, what's wrong?" Parai placed her mug to her lips and stared at me with those big, pretty eyes of hers.

"What isn't wrong is the better question. I got my fiancée chewing my head off because she constantly feels the need to overstep her boundaries and come for my son's mother. The crazy part about it is that Rosé ain't even the one starting all the trouble: Zarielle is. She got me feeling like I made the wrong choice when I chose her over Rosé."

"So then why are you with her?"

I took a sip of tea, trying to find the perfect lie because the truth was too much. "I'm with Zarielle because it's the right thing to do. She's loyal to a fault and that's a hard thing to find nowadays."

"Rosé can't be loyal to you? She's running your shop and bringing in crazy clientele. I haven't seen her do a single disloyal thing." Parai cocked her head to the side and asked, "Would you like to tell me the real reason or am I gonna have to give you some more whiskey?"

"Zarielle has done shit for me that no other woman has and no other woman ever will. She's gone places that I wouldn't even expect… if she can show me that loyalty then why not return it?"

"Do you love her?"

The question gave me pause. The hate and bitterness Zarielle had just shown me caused me to think twice before answering. I couldn't even see myself leaving her alone with Cago for fear that she might not treat him right. Are these thoughts you're supposed to have about someone that you love and plan to spend the rest of your life with? As of right now, I wasn't sure where we stood, whether I still wanted to marry her, child or not. Parai's expression went from curious to knowing the longer I sat there. After five minutes passed and I still couldn't formulate the words, did she hold her hands up in defeat.

"I'm not about to have you out here lying to me when these are real questions that you have to ask yourself. You answer that question when you're ready to," she said, placing her mug on the table and reaching underneath the couch. She set the book bag I had given to her this morning on the couch between us. "I know that I asked you for this opportunity because I wanted to pay my bills and make sure that I was straight, but I took a look at what's inside of here and had to ask myself whether or not this was a lifestyle I wanted to get into. I'll get the money for school, but not like this. I hope you're not mad."

"I'm actually feeling the exact opposite—you too good for this. You got goals and dreams that go beyond this. The last thing you wanna do is mess that up chasing money that ain't even worth it. Trust me, if I didn't have so many responsibilities, I'd go back to my clean lifestyle."

"You quit the game?"

"With no intention of getting back into it. Then life came and hit me with a one-two punch. I got a kid, another one on the way, and a fiancée that wants the world. A little tattoo shop ain't paying for all of that."

"If you keep up that mentality then it won't," Parai said, placing a comforting hand on my thigh. "The same way you're hustling in the streets to make ends meet is the same way you roll your sleeves up and start making a name for yourself in the industry you want to be a part of. Sometimes you gotta bet on yourself."

Somewhere in the middle her speech, Parai and I had subconsciously closed the space between us. She was so close that I could see the flecks of green in her hazel eyes. All I had to do was lean in and—

"What are you thinking?" Parai breathed, breaking the trance I was in.

"Your words…they reminded me of someone."

"Whoever she is, she sounds like she loves you." She didn't have to say it out loud, but I knew Parai was telling me to back my ass up before I did something I'd likely regret later.

I leaned back and finished off my mug of tea. "You're absolutely right. One day she might be able to forgive me and I don't wanna fuck things up between the two of us." I continued thinking about Rosé and a thought came to mind. "I know you were apprehensive about tattooing, but I think I have an idea for how you can make that money to pay your tuition."

"There's something about listening to you that makes me trust you. I'm down for whatever you wanna do, Shacago, make me your canvas," Parai said with a smile.

Everything about Parai made me think about Rosé and how

much I missed being with her. Her words in the parking lot were what made me fall in love with her and maybe, just maybe, I could use that love to find what I'm really looking for.

******

After setting up an early morning meeting with Parai, it was time to hang out with Cago. I was so busy being mad at Zarielle that I forgot to pack some clothes for the weekend. I wasn't in the mood to argue with Zarielle, but I promised myself I would be in and out. My plans went right out the window when I walked through the door and found Zarielle sitting at the table waiting for me, except this time she was dressed in a red teddy holding a glass of scotch.

"Shacago, as soon as you walked out the door I thought about how unfair I was being to you," Zarielle said, staring at her clear stripper shoes like a shy, little girl. "When I accepted your ring, I promised to love you unconditionally, baby mother or not. I know I haven't been the best to deal with, but I still have Angelica on my mind and being back at the shop I started thinking about her—"

"Baby, you ain't gotta explain nothing else," I said, covering her with kisses and guiding her over to the table set for two. "I didn't think about how being back there since Angelica was killed might've made you feel. I'm sorry for not taking your feelings into consideration and making you feel like you weren't a part of our relationship."

Zarielle pushed me into my seat and straddled me, her mysterious eyes leaving mine only to pick up the plate of food next to us. "I wasn't sure how long you were gonna be gone, so I made one of your easiest favorites: grilled steak with hand whipped mashed potatoes and broccoli. Sit back, my handsome king, and lemme take good care of you."

I wasn't one of them niggas that liked being waited on hand and foot—my pops put my mother through enough of that shit when I was little—but when Zarielle did it, I felt like it was her showing me the ultimate respect for everything I was doing. Sometimes she has her moments where I'm left wondering where we stand and then she does something amazing like this, killing any second thoughts I had. I started thinking about the conversation I had with Parai and knew this was the reason why I couldn't answer whether or not I loved her.

What we had at this point went beyond love.

I can only think of a handful of women that would put up with everything Zarielle does for me. She's been standing by my side despite everything thrown on my plate. From me becoming a father to me financially trying to make ends meet. Was it the same love that I shared for Rosé?

No, but it was good enough.

CHAPTER 5

Momma's Baby Daddy's Maybe

Rosé

"Girl, I don't see anyone showing up to this last-minute barbeque you over here tryna throw," Candice said, sipping her wine while I prepped the steaks for the grill. "If even ten people showed up, I'd be in shock. How about this? Instead of playing coy you tell me what's really going on here?"

I stopped prepping and sagged my shoulders. "Shacago's coming. Marquise is too. This will be the first time they'll be in the same room since Marquise and I made it official. Whether or not they can get along today will tell me if this relationship's going to work."

"Why wouldn't they be able to get along?"

"The way Shacago's pride is set up…"

"Ooooh. You didn't tell him about—"

"Nope, I haven't thought about a proper way to tell him," I said, taking a deep breath. "You think it'll be bad?"

Candice dramatically gazed upward and said, "Yeah, it's going to end real ugly, but look on the bright side—at least you're pretty."

"Candice…"

"Listen, Rosé," Candice started, holding me by the shoulders, "you can't allow someone to get mad at you for wanting the better life for yourself that you deserve. It's not like you're trying to create a new family like he did. Shacago made his choice and now he's gotta live with it, okay?"

"You're absolutely right, you are absolutely right…"

Any butterflies I had in my stomach disappeared, and I went back to setting up for my party. Candice and I put on the last finishing touches to our housewarming barbecue when everyone started to arrive. Raven and Parai arrived first, bearing the Bordeaux KitchenAid mixer I had been drooling over to go with the burgundy and white color scheme of our kitchen; Suede and Kidd showed up with their twins and a couple bottles of Möet (I didn't expect any less coming from those two); and Elijah and his wife, Tracey, showed up with their son, Neil, and a nice cutlery set. We were on to the second bottle of champagne when Shacago and Zarielle walked in with Xavier lagging behind in order to make his own entrance.

"Wassup, big sis!" Xavier exclaimed, holding up two more bottles of champagne in one hand—this time Ace of Spades. "You already know I had to come out and celebrate with you!"

"Thanks, X," I said, hugging him and accepting the bottles. "Is

64

that your girlfriend?"

Xavier turned to see a girl no older than eighteen enter the apartment with her lip poked out. He must've left the poor girl behind and didn't even bother to properly introduce her. "Oh, yeah, this is my newest honey, Gabi. Gabi, this is my big sister, Rosé, Cago's mom."

"Nice to meet you," Gabi said, extending her hand to shake mine. She turned to Shacago and shot him a look of approval. "You had some good taste."

Had?

Raven and Candice exchanged surprised faces while Parai took her glass of champagne to the head. Shacago's only been here for five minutes and it's already going left. I wanted to give Gabi a high-five, but that would make the drama become worse.

Zarielle was about to spit some venom from her mouth when I butted in and asked, "Where's my baby at?"

"He's on his way with Little X and Yandi," Shacago said, ushering Zarielle into the party and away from Gabi, who stood there with the biggest smirk on her face. "Where should I put our gift?"

"Right there on that table." I pointed to the hall table packed with gifts and turned my attention back to Xavier once they were out of earshot. "X, what the fuck was that all about?" I mouthed, stating between Gabi, who had begun mingling, to Zarielle, who was watching the young girl like she wanted to pop off. "Them bitches got beef or something? Because I don't got time to be putting away my good shit if they decide to scrap."

Xavier waved off my worries. "They had a disagreement a while ago and never spoke their piece. Don't worry; I got Gabi under control, aight? We ain't gon' fuck up your turn up."

"That's all I wanted to know," I said, kissing him on the cheek and going back to hosting.

Elijah was out on the balcony grilling the steaks with Tracey, who was acting as his helper. While his loving wife was having a good time, Eli seemed distracted. I knew what this was about and addressed it before he could find something to say.

"Special Agent in Charge Eli, there's nothing to worry about. I told Xavier to keep his girlfriend in check and he promised me that he would. Now stop worrying about them and get to making my steaks."

My gentle slap on the arm was enough for Eli to snap out of the trance he was in. "Sorry, I was just thinking about some work stuff. Nothing important."

I glanced in the house to see Shacago talking with Parai and turned back to Elijah. "You aren't still pursuing Shacago, are you?"

"Rosé, the last person on my mind right now is Cago's father. The agency has bigger fish to fry and speaking of bigger fish, one just walked right through the door."

Marquise was greeted with the usual hoopla that surrounded him after being made into an instant celebrity. No matter how many daps or hugs he handed out, it didn't stop him from pulling me into a kiss that left no questions on whether or not we were together. There was a wolf whistle or two, which I tried to ignore, but my face turned red anyway. Marquise liked the attention as much as he liked having me on his arm.

"I'm glad you made it," I said, guiding him into the kitchen once the hype died down. "I want you to meet my brother and his family."

"Damn, you got a nigga real nervous. I haven't met the family of a woman I'm seeing since…since their daddy could threaten to whip my ass and have it be a viable threat."

"Come on," I said, pulling him towards the balcony. "Stop being—"

"MOMMY!"

I stumbled a bit when Cago went plummeting into me, his arms wrapping around me, and squeezing tight. A month had passed since Shacago started getting him every weekend and my baby always came home acting like he couldn't live without me. I couldn't even lie, every time he came home and covered me in kisses, I felt complete. Stealing a peek at Marquise, I knew exactly what I had to do. Although we hadn't been seeing each other that long, things were serious and the two of them meeting was bound to happen.

"Cago, there's someone I want you to meet," I said, standing up and taking Marquise's hand. "This is Marquise, my—"

"Boyfriend? The one you're always talking about on the phone with Auntie Raven?" Cago said with a sly smile.

I felt my cheeks heat up even more as Marquise started laughing. He knelt and held out his hand to Cago. "Nice to meet you, Cago. Since everyone brought your moms and Candice a nice gift, I figured I would get you a housewarming gift. It's upstairs waiting for you."

"What do you say?" I said to Cago, who was bobbing excitedly on his heels.

Cago shook his hand. "Thank you, Marquise."

"Go 'head and enjoy, little man," Marquise said, laughing as Cago dashed out the kitchen, calling for Neil and Little X to follow him. "I hope your brother is just as easy to win over, Rosé."

"Maybe with a couple tickets to your next fight I might approve," Elijah said from the balcony doorway. He opened his arms and greeted Marquise like he was an old family friend, which was a surprise to me because he only regarded Shacago with mild interest. "Nice to meet you, man. Rosé's been telling us all about you."

Tracey entered the kitchen bearing a plate of steaks, her brows cocked at her husband. "I see someone got excited about Marquise being here and left me to take the steaks off the grill."

"I'm sorry, baby," Elijah said, kissing her on the forehead and grabbing the plate. "Marquise this is the love of my life and my wife, Tracey."

While Marquise made small talk with my family, I went to catch up with Yandi, who brought along Quan and what looked to be some of his goons. I stole a glance at Xavier, who took Gabi by the hand and led her out onto the balcony. Shacago and I shared a look before I greeted Yandi, who was dressed in a cute Dior piece.

"Girl, look at you," I said, holding her at an arm's length and making her spin around so I could get a good look at the powder pink skirt and shirt with matching boots. "Coming up in here looking like money."

"That's how we do," Quan said before placing a possessive arm around her waist and pulling her close. "Wassup, Rosé."

"Hey, Quan, Quan's people," I said, figuring that stunting was something they did regularly but showing up with a gift might be too much. "Y'all get comfortable and enjoy the food."

"Baby, I'mma make you a plate, okay?" Yandi said, pulling me towards the balcony where I'm sure she saw Xavier disappear to. "Girl, this place is amazing. I know you getting real well known, but you gotta have a couple of coins to rub together to get a nice place like this."

"I had some help," I replied, keeping it as vague as possible just in case someone was listening. "How was Cago?"

"He's such a sweetie pie. He wanted to know if he could stay the week with us. I promise to make sure he doesn't get into any trouble with them neighborhood kids. Please, Rosé?"

"Alright, he can come back with you for this week. That'll give me some time to get the rest of the house together. Yandi?"

Yandi stopped paying me attention and was now staring down Xavier and Gabi, who were making out against the balcony railing. I could feel the shit she was about to try and start vibrating through the air. I tossed a plate of potato salad together along with some rice, a fresh steak, and a shish kabob and handed it to her.

"Didn't you come out here to get your man some food? Here you go. Now carry your ass back in there," I said, giving her a playful pat on the butt and pushing her towards the doorway. "Be good."

"Yeah, be good," Shacago said jokingly as he stepped outside. "You got a real nice party going on, Rosé. Thanks for the invite."

"You're welcome. You know I couldn't leave you out of the festivities," I said, bobbing on my heels. "I put a steak aside to cook for you when you got here. I know you like yours medium and no one has ever been able to make them right."

"Aww shit, I'm about to get one of Rosé's famous steaks? Shit, lemme pull up my chair and take notes on this." Shacago grabbed a chair from the table and sat a few feet away. "I see your family is feelin' Marquise. They in there having a good old time talking like they known each other for years."

"I'm just as surprised as you are," I said, heating up the grill and getting to work on two steaks—one for Shacago and one for Marquise. "Most importantly, Cago likes him, which is a relief."

"Where is Cago?"

"Marquise bought him a housewarming gift and I haven't seen him or the boys since."

"Okay," Shacago said and I could hear the unspoken words in his tone of voice. "This is a real nice spot you got here. I thought the place y'all looked at was on Dekalb and Throop?"

"It was, but that was our second choice and this one was our first, but we couldn't get it because it was way too expensive."

The steaks hit the grill and made a loud sizzling noise, adding to the tension I felt radiating off Shacago. I hummed a tune as I worked on the steaks, thinking about how to just come out with the truth. It was now or never and the worst that could happen is that he gets mad. It won't change the situation, but at least I won't feel like I have to hide the big, pink elephant in the room.

"Shacago, I need to tell you something."

"What?"

I was about to come out with it when Marquise, Elijah, and Tracey came onto the balcony with Candice following behind. Could this get any worse, I thought as I flipped the steaks and prepared to take them off the grill.

"What are you two up to out here?" Candice asked, taking a sip of champagne and stealing a glance at Shacago.

"Nothing, I was just waiting to hear what Rosé was gonna tell me about y'all spot."

"Oh, you mean how I bought it?" Marquise said casually. "I knew Rosé wanted a nice spot in her old neighborhood, so I made it happen."

"Word?" Shacago replied, rubbing his goatee as he kept his eyes on me, waiting for me to look away from the steaks and acknowledge him. "How much this spot run you?"

"I don't even know. I gave Rosé a blank check and let her handle it. Baby, how much was this place?"

"It was $979,500," I said, pulling the steaks off the grill and placing them on a plate. "Shacago, you ready for your steak?"

"Can I speak to you alone for a minute?" Shacago stood up from his seat and went back inside.

"Did I say something wrong?" Marquise asked, motioning to the spot where Shacago was sitting.

Candice popped her lips and replied, "You actually might've said something right."

Once I made sure Marquise was squared away and good with my

brother, I went to find Shacago, who was standing at the bottom of the staircase with his arms crossed. I beckoned for him to follow me upstairs to my bedroom. We passed Cago's room, where he and the boys were playing one of the five brand new game consoles Marquise surprised Cago with. I heard Shacago suck his teeth and knew that was more ammo. I hadn't even closed my bedroom door when he started.

"This nigga bought you a whole entire house?" Shacago said incredulously. "A nigga you been fucking with for two months' tops is out here buying you a house? What's next, a car?" My silence was a confirmation to his question. "What kind of car?"

"A Range Rover," I said in a small voice. "He doesn't want me taking Ubers all the time or waiting to borrow Candice's car. It wasn't my intention to accept his gifts but—"

"But what? You gon' throw the nigga some pussy to see how much more you can get?"

I bristled at his remark. "Excuse me? I know you ain't just accuse me of doing the same shit your fiancée been doing long before y'all got together: selling her pussy to whoever could afford it."

"Don't talk about Zarielle like—"

"I'll talk about Zarielle however I damn well please in my fucking house when you tryna sit here and call me a whore because my man likes to make sure I'm taken care of." I let off a harsh laugh. "Is that what this is all about? You're jealous because your $30,000 wasn't good enough to buy what I pictured for our son? Well, guess what? Marquise paid for this place with LEGITIMATE MONEY! That's why my brother can sit down there and laugh with him because he doesn't have to worry about the

Feds arresting me behind some bullshit. I don't have to stress out about the roof over my son's head being seized because it was paid for with dirty money!"

"Once upon a time, that dirty money was good enough for you! It treated you right when your father kicked you out and you was living on the streets. My lifestyle fed you more times than you'll ever be able to count and always made sure you had somewhere to shit and lay your head. You used to be a real ride-or-die, Rosé. A woman that I could blindly trust with my life. What the fuck happened to you?" Shacago asked with disgust.

I closed the space between us and said through gritted teeth, "I got pregnant by a man on his way to jail and decided that not only should I want better, but do better."

"So, this is better?" Shacago said, waving his hand at the entire house. "You better than me?" I opened my mouth to reply when he cut me off with a brusque, "Don't even answer that. I came here to not only tell you that I had made enough to get out the game, but I also wanted to collab on this full body piece I planned to do on Parai. It was supposed to show our unity after everything we been through. I been drawing it up every spare chance I get and I wanted to show you tomorrow, but obviously since I ain't nothing but a fucking simple ass criminal that you regret fucking, maybe we ain't as united as I thought we were."

"Shacago—"

"Save that shit for your nigga downstairs," Shacago said, brushing past me and opening the door. He turned and said, "Just so you know, I would've never made you feel that small in front of people."

The door slammed, scaring me hard enough that the tears I was holding back spilled. I had done more than hurt Shacago—I bruised his pride and left him looking like half a man in front of everyone. My intentions weren't to hurt him. I was just trying to get a piece of the happiness he's always been blessed with.

Xavier

"Zarielle, we out," I heard Shacago say from the living room. "I'll see all of you at work tomorrow. Make sure you ain't late either."

I pulled Gabi back into the living room in time to see Shacago and Zarielle's exiting backs as Rosé hit the first floor landing looking visibly upset. She wiped her eyes, fanned them, and rejoined the party like nothing happened. I was happy with Shacago and Rosé's dissent; it was the only way I could keep Shacago right where I wanted him. Yet, there was something about the look on Rosé's face that made me feel the need to comfort her.

"You wanna talk about it in the kitchen?"

Rosé opened her mouth to reply when Yandi popped up out of nowhere and guided Rosé to the kitchen. Gabi, being the understanding girlfriend that she was, went and joined Rosé's friend that worked at the shop. I found Rosé crying on Yandi's shoulder while Yandi patted her back uncomfortably. *This bitch scared to mess up her one nice outfit,* I thought immediately.

"Yo, why you snatch her away like that when you saw me about to talk to her?" I asked, placing my hand in my pocket so Yandi wouldn't try to have me looking like the bad guy with a Fed in the building.

Yandi scoffed. "I snatched her because you need to be talking to your bitch ass brother about coming here just to start trouble. But I forgot—that's all the Stanfield brothers are good for."

"I'm over here tryna look out for Rosé and all you doing is making it about yourself, which is why I got rid of your bum ass!"

Rosé stepped out of Yandi's arms and placed her own between us. "Can y'all please not fight right now? I had enough of arguing for tonight."

"As soon as your cousin knock that shit off. What you think 'cause you came up in here in last season's Dior on and a wannabe thug ass nigga that you can talk to me however you want?"

"My man already owes you an ass whupping! Don't have him cash a check your ass can't afford to write!" Yandi shouted, poking her chest out and acting like her shit ain't stink.

Quan rushed into the kitchen with his niggas in tow, pushed Rosé into Yandi, and had his chest pressed against mine before I could plant my feet. I took a couple steps back but I snapped back, pressing that nigga and giving him the eye. There was a slight commotion behind us and Shacago's niggas were at my side squared up and ready to go.

"Nigga, back the fuck up out my face!" I shouted, my jaw working as I fought with all my strength to keep from pulling out my piece and ending this nigga. "Check ya fucking bitch before I slap the shit outta her ass again!"

"You ain't doing a motherfucking thing," Quan said and got this crazed look in his eye. "Are you?"

I suddenly felt hot—my head started spinning and all I could hear was my blood pumping through my veins. My hand started reaching for my piece when I remembered how much I wanted to torture this nigga before I put a bullet in his head. Rosé's brother, Elijah, came into the kitchen with her man in tow.

"What the hell is going on in here?" Elijah said, hands on his waist, his brows raised, looking like every bit of the Fed that he was.

Quan and I backed off each other at the same time, allowing me to save face. At the sight of the Feds, his boys were already looking nervous and ready to go, which they did once Quan grabbed Yandi's hand and started pulling her out of the kitchen.

"Yandi, get your kid so we can leave," Quan shouted.

Quan may have been able to half punk me in front of everyone over Yandi, but there was no way in hell they were taking my son anywhere with these foul ass niggas.

"You ain't taking my son nowhere!" I shouted, following them out the kitchen and down the hall with the men following behind me while the women stayed behind.

Quan looked ready to argue when Elijah checked it brusquely, "Yandi, I don't know what's gotten into you, but you aren't taking Xavier home tonight! Remember, I'm not your boyfriend or your baby daddy! Your momma gave me permission to check your ass however I see fit! So, take your boyfriend and get out!"

Yandi shot me a death glare and tugged Quan, "C'mon, let's get out of here."

"Nigga, tonight is your lucky night," Quan said, shooting up his middle finger while his niggas started shouting out what set they represented. "You ain't gon' have a pig backing you up out on the streets."

"My number is 347-555-4012," I shot back. "Pick a place, nigga, and I'll be there."

There was no playing around with this nigga anymore. He was taking me out of character, and for that, I'mma have to put him in a casket.

CHAPTER 6

Paid in Full

Shacago

"What the fuck happened up there?" Zarielle asked as we exited the building. "One minute everything was fine, I was having a good time with the twins, and the next you're storming out of the party like a little kid."

"Some bullshit," I said, pressing the button on my keychain to locate my car, watching it light up halfway down the black. "Marquise paid for Rosé's house after I gave her money to pay for the other place she wanted."

"He bought her a whole house? After only two months? Sounds like somebody's looking for a come up and a new daddy for your son. We might have to take this to court, Shacago," Zarielle said, pulling her phone from her purse and waving it back and forth. "I've been looking at some stuff online about you possibly getting joint custody. Once we get our house I have no problem with having Cago living there half the time."

Over the past four weekends that I had Cago, he'd become pretty tight with Zarielle. I wasn't sure whether it was pregnancy or the fact that us becoming a family was becoming more real, but Zarielle was embracing my extended family without a problem. For her to be so proactive about making sure we became a unit, convinced me that, once again, I made the right choice.

"That's exactly what I feel like doing. How's my son gon' look at me if another man's providing for him?"

We were nearly at the car when a commotion broke out behind us. Quan, Yandi, and Quan's entourage came flying out of Rosé's building. Somewhere in the midst of the noise, was an argument going on between Quan and Yandi.

"Why is that I always find you in the middle of some bullshit with that nigga? I keep you in the best shit, give you the opportunity to be on my arm when I could've had plenty of other bitches, and deal with the kid you got by a bum ass nigga! Even with all of that, I still gotta drag you away from petty ass project shit! What the fuck is wrong with you, Yandi?"

"Ain't shit wrong with me, but I'm sure there's something wrong with your bitch ass! You claim to be a big badass nigga and when I rep that shit you acting like it's a problem! Either you a hard ass nigga or maybe I need to go back up there with my baby father 'cause that nigga don't back down from nobody."

Quan cocked his fist back and punched Yandi dead in the face. Yandi's head reeled back and she hit the floor with a thud. I was pissed at Rosé, but I wasn't about to let a nigga put his hands on her family. Even Zarielle didn't try to stop me as I ran back down the block. One of Quan's friends caught sight of me and moved like he was ready to pop off.

"You like putting your hands on women? Come and put them on me. Y'all wanna fight, too? Line up and square the fuck up!" I shouted, walking up to the one ready nigga, grabbing him by the neck, and knocking him out with a skull crack. "And if a one-on-one is a problem for you pussy ass niggas, we can solve this shit another way."

I pulled out my piece and placed it to Quan's chest. His hitters stepped up to the plate and placed their guns to my head. That cockiness that was in Quan's eyes ebbed and faded; this nigga already knew that I wasn't about pulling my piece for show. I was about to use it with no hesitation. Fuck Rosé, fuck the police, and fuck her Fed fucking brother upstairs. Yandi jumped up off the floor like she had been electrocuted and grabbed my hand.

"What the fuck are you doing, Shacago?" she screamed, pushing Quan back and placing herself at the end of my gun.

"What the fuck am I doing? What your pops ain't here to do! When X used to put his hands on you I checked him for that shit, so you think that was gon' change with the next nigga?"

"This is all your fault anyway! Now you wanna fuck up the night even more? Just get outta here and let me handle my business."

I removed my gun from Yandi's chest and put it away. "If I ever find out that this is going on while my nephew is around, Xavier will be the least of your problems."

Yandi knew I meant business, which was why she wove her arm through Quan's and pulled him down the block. His hittas lowered their guns and stepped off, leaving me standing there with my chest heaving. If it wasn't Rosé fucking up the flow, then it was Xavier ending up in the middle of some bullshit that had nothing to do with him. I was in desperate need of a break, and if I didn't get one, then I was likely to lose my mind.

"What happened back there?" Zarielle asked, craning her neck to get a good look at the group as we drove past them. "All I saw was guns go up and then they went down. I'm assuming niggas remembered who they were fucking with and changed it up real quick."

"They figured it out with the help of Yandi," I confirmed, not even bothering to spare them clowns a glance. "Zarielle?"

"Yes, baby?"

"I know you had your heart set on planning a big, fancy wedding, but I was thinking what if we packed our shit up and went somewhere real beautiful? México, the Bahamas, the Dominican Republic, wherever you want. We go and get married."

Zarielle jumped up and down excitedly, slapping my arm and kissing me on the cheek. "A destination wedding? That's exactly what I wanted! Ugh, this is gonna be so exciting. I don't even know what to pick and where to start…"

"Don't worry about the dollar amount. You already know it's whatever you like."

******

I showed up to the shop the next day in a good mood despite

last night's events. My entire team wasted no time cluing me into what happened after I left. Honestly, I wasn't the least bit surprised by the fact that a fight broke out. Yandi went out of her way to get under Xavier's skin, but I was surprised that my brother didn't beat the dog shit out of Quan. Xavier wasn't someone to back down from a fight, and when it came to somebody disrespecting him, he didn't take it lightly. Thinking about his recent attack and the amount of men that Quan ran with, I came to the conclusion that the culprits were closer than I thought. This left me asking myself one valid question.

Why is Xavier letting these niggas breathe?

"Good morning, boss," Parai said with a bat of her eyelashes. "I hope you're feeling much better today than you were yesterday."

"I'm good," I replied, taking a peek over her shoulder at the appointments for today. She smelled like her usual lavender and something sweet…like honey. She faced me and we were barely inches apart, our noses brushing from the close proximity. One false move and—

"That's good. I don't like to see you upset," Parai replied huskily before returning her attention to the appointment book, jotting down notes as if the intimate moment didn't happen.

I tried to play it cool, scratching the back of my neck and asking, "Rosé come in today?"

"She's in the back sleeping off a serious hangover. After the fight ended and Quan left, we turned all the way up. I didn't even think I would make it in today."

"I'm glad to see your dedication. Do me a favor and bring the whole crew into my office in like ten minutes," I told her before heading to my office, where I found Rosé laid out on the couch with a fur coat over her head.

I slammed the door shut and smiled when Rosé jumped and snatched the coat off her head. The light made her think twice and she pulled it back over her head, groaning the entire time.

"You don't get paid to lay around," I reminded her as I took a seat in the chair behind me.

"You don't pay me at all."

I dug in my pocket and peeled off two stacks. I yanked her coat off her head and tossed the cash onto her stomach. "Consider this your first bi-weekly payment."

"Shacago, I'm not in the mood to play tit-for-tat with you. What do you want?"

"I need to talk to you about a couple things. First, we gotta talk about what happened after I left last night."

"You mean when your brother and Quan almost had a shootout in the middle of my kitchen? For the first time in recent history, I can actually say this wasn't Xavier's fault. That little maggot is gonna be the death of Yandi if she doesn't leave him alone. I know it's hard out there, but why is it that all she can ever bring home is these crazy ass thugs?"

"Add abusive to the equation and I agree 100%." Rosé sat up and I told her, "Last night Quan beat her ass and I almost blew his head off his shoulders before she jumped in the middle and acted like this was all my fault. Rosé, I'ont know what he's doing for your cousin, but you need to get her mind right and get her away from him before I gotta take matters into my own hands and handle him since Xavier moving real funny around that nigga. I ain't never seen him act like this with anyone and I'm ready to press him about it."

"You know how Xavier is with people that he hates—he starts plotting on them. Quan's a cocky motherfucker, so I can guarantee you that X is just waiting for him to slip up. Honestly…I think we all are."

"What that nigga do to you for you to hate him?" Rosé wasn't Miss Congeniality, but you had to dig deep under her skin for her to wish death on you.

"He's got fucked up vibes, but enough about his bitch ass. What else did you need to talk to me about?" Rosé asked, already looking tired from a conversation with Yandi she hadn't even had yet.

"I'm about to make an announcement and I need your undivided attention," I said as the door opened and everyone started filing in. "Fam, I called you all in here to share some good news. Zarielle and I wanted to invite you to our wedding in Punta Cana. We're covering everything, including the airfare. All y'all need to worry about is showing up and having a passport."

Everyone started whooping and hollering until Rosé broke it up with, "When is this wedding supposed to be happening?"

"This weekend."

Excitement continued to fill the room with everyone congratulating me and asking me a million questions at once. Rosé shot me a withering look before walking out the door. She had to be crazy if she thought I was about to follow her especially after the shit she pulled last night. I guess she ain't know these games are for two players.

Rosé

"I can't believe he's getting married this weekend and that you're actually entertaining the thought of going," Candice said as we lay in my bed, eating a tub of Häagen-Dazs. "Unless the reason you're going is to object. In which case, let's start shopping for the perfect 'I object' dress."

"I'm not going to object. I know I didn't have much time to tell you about the argument I had with Shacago, but I think it's really over between us. This argument was different; it showed how much we've grown up and grown apart over the past seven years. Every time life gets tough, Shacago turns to the streets, and I can't deal with someone who only has one solution when life gets hard. Marquise is proof that you can take care of yourself with your talents."

"Marquise came from money, Rosé. That's like comparing apples and oranges. The people in his life supported his decision to box and helped him become successful. Please show me one person other than yourself that encourages Shacago to tat?"

"That doesn't matter! If you love something enough then you'll do it regardless of what people say, and that's a lesson Shacago hasn't learned yet. He's going to always feed the streets and I can't deal with that anymore."

The doorbell interrupted our conversation, ringing through the halls and letting me know that Yandi had finally arrived to pick up

Little X. This would be the perfect time for me to have a talk with her without—

"Quan," I said, opening the door and allowing the last person I wanted to see inside of my home. "What are you doing here? Where's Yandi?"

"The salon was busy so she sent me over here to pick up Little X. I know yesterday wasn't the best impression you got of me, but I wanted to apologize and tell you that I ain't mean to disrespect your house like that."

I gave him a complacent shrug. "I'm sure you do a lot of shit you don't mean to do—like put your hands on my cousin. I heard about what you did after y'all left the party and I don't play that shit. You need to leave my cousin alone."

"Your cousin was asking for that," Quan said, taking a menacing step towards me. "I'm giving Yandi all of me and all she ever gives in return is some drama with a nigga she claims she over. To be honest, you're right—I should leave Yandi alone. But then I ain't got nobody to replace her with. Not all of us are as lucky as Marquise."

I cocked my head to the side. "Excuse me?"

"I been playing it real cool while Yandi's around, but a nigga really feeling you. You can fuck with this boxing nigga for right now 'cause he making a couple moves I ain't even mad at, but I'm about to take over these streets and when I do, I'mma need a bad bitch by my side."

"And you're telling me this because?" I pinched the bridge of my nose. "This really can't be happening. You didn't come with the sole purpose of picking up Little X, did you? This was the smoothest way you could make a move on me while my cousin is eating all the bullshit you can feed her. I would hold Little X until she comes to get him, but that's not going to stop you from being around him. LITTLE X!"

Little X came running downstairs with Cago in tow. He didn't appear to be fazed by the sight of Quan—if I would've caught even a whiff of fear or discomfort he wouldn't be going anywhere. Quan's jaw was working like he wanted to give me a piece of his mind over my choice words for his fuck boy shenanigans, but he kept it shut for the sake of the kids.

"Hey, little man," Quan said, ruffling Little X's short, curly fro. "I'm dropping you off at your mom's salon. Wanna get some McDonald's on the way there?"

"Yay! See you later, Cago and Auntie Rosé!" Little X said, hugging us and making his way to the door.

"See y'all later," Quan said and puckered his lips at me.

I rolled my eyes. "See you later, Little X! Tell Mommy to call me, okay?"

Once they were gone, I locked the door and leaned against it. Closing my eyes, I wondered if things could get any worse. I felt Cago's arms wrap around my waist, and it was moments like these that I cherished.

"I don't know what's wrong, Mommy, but it's going to get better. I promise," Cago said, giving me a gentle squeeze.

"It got better with you, baby, and as long as you're here, it'll always be good."

******

After a pep talk from Raven, a bottle of wine from Candice, and a night of loving from Marquise, who was supportive of my decision to attend the wedding, I was lying on a beach in the Dominican Republic admiring the clear blue water. Fuck this wedding—since I was on a getaway I was going to stay away from this drama. While everyone was enjoying the wedding festivities, I was kicking back and relaxing by myself.

"So, you came all the way to another country to be antisocial?" an amused voice said from above me.

I lowered my sunglasses to find Parai standing over me. She took a seat, allowing me to get a good look at her amazing body and luminous, brown skin. It was sparkling in the sunlight and earning her looks from everyone that walked by. I felt a pang in my chest at losing the opportunity to ink her with Shacago.

"I came here because Shacago wanted our son to be in this wedding, and there was no way in hell I was allowing my baby to come to another country without me. I can promise you that Shacago is happy that I'm not around to kill everyone's vibes."

"I wouldn't say 'happy,' but your absence has been noted a few times," Parai replied. "Are you going to tell Shacago how you feel about him?"

I placed my sunglasses back on my face and replied, "I'm not about to walk down that road again, Parai. I think Shacago and I know where we stand."

It was true; other than discussing Cago and the shop, Shacago and I barely said a word to each other. He was busy planning his last-minute wedding and I was having the time of my life with Cago and Marquise, who played the role of "fun boyfriend" to the tee. The Dominican Republic wasn't ideal, but it was a nice way to end such a wonderful week. Shacago became a fleeting thought, which told me all I needed to know about our future.

"So, you're going to let him marry Zarielle for all the wrong reasons? When I asked him whether or not he loved her, he couldn't give me a straight answer. You know what that says, right?"

"That Shacago likes being a byproduct of his environment. Parai, Shacago's far from dumb. I'm sure he wouldn't marry Zarielle unless he really felt something for her."

"Maybe he's marrying her because he knows that eventually you and Marquise will get married," Parai said, turning on her side and staring at me head on. "That's what it's looking like."

"What am I supposed to do? Ask him why he's getting married and if I don't like the answer then what?"

"That's for you to figure out, but I think you owe it to yourself to figure it out before Shacago walks down the aisle."

"Fine, Parai," I grumbled, closing my eyes and thinking about her words.

I must've been thinking really hard because I woke up to a dark and partially empty beach. People were still having fun, but it was a different kind of fun. Fires were burning, music was playing, and people were partying. Checking my phone, I saw that it was nearly ten o'clock at night and no one bothered to check up on me, not even

Candice, who came along as my support system.

"Some support system," I mumbled under my breath as I opened the door to my suite. Candice was sitting at the vanity applying her makeup. "What have you been doing all day other than abandoning your best friend?"

"Girl, someone had to get the tea since you were acting all sullen and lonely," Candice replied easily as she applied her lipstick. "I was hanging with everyone, playing cute and friendly long enough to find out Shacago's momma isn't feeling this union at all. She said she's going to support her son regardless of what he does, but it's obvious who Shacago's supposed to be walking down the aisle with."

"Mom said that?" I said with thinly veiled disbelief. "What did you say back?"

"I told her that if I have my way this wedding won't be taking place tomorrow night."

"Oh really," I replied dryly, tired of feeling all this pressure on my shoulders to make things right with Shacago when half of this was his fault. "Tell me, how do you plan to make that happen?"

Candice spun in her seat and blew me a kiss. "Easy. We're going to crash his bachelor party."

******

Ass. Ass. Ass.

Twerking on the tables and shaking in front of every man in the room. Taking in the big Dominican booties, I now understood why everyone was coming to the country to build a body. Major Lazer's

"Bubble Butt" was blasting through the speakers of the hotel suite. Raven, Candice, and I were the only fully dressed women, leading me to believe Zarielle and her crew was off getting into some fun of their own.

"There he is over there," Raven said, pointing to a secluded corner where I could vaguely make out Shacago with two strippers. "Good luck, girl."

"I don't need any luck because I can see this ending rather quickly," I replied before balling up my hands and strutting over to Shacago and his hoes.

I wasn't sure who these strippers thought I was, but I brought out the best in them. Their ass shaking intensified and I was impressed. Shacago took his eyes off the ass he was immersed in and locked with mine, sipping from the bottle of Ace of Spades clutched tightly.

"Can I talk to you for a minute?" I said, crossing my arms and tapping my foot.

Shacago motioned to the strippers and replied, "I don't know whether or not you noticed, but I'm in the middle of something."

"Shacago—"

"Come on, let's get this over with."

I wasn't in the mood for his games and he must've noticed because he extracted himself from the dancers and motioned for me to follow him out onto the balcony. The sky was clear and the moon was shining brightly. I found myself stargazing, admiring the tiny bright dots that peppered the sky.

"You call me out here to stare up at the sky or to have a conversation?" Shacago asked, taking a swig of his champagne and standing next to me.

I shot him a glance and said, "I came out here to talk about what happened earlier this week."

"Rosé, tonight's my last night of freedom and you over here tryna weigh me down and shit. That ain't cool..."

"I'm just trying to make sure that you're doing this for all the right reasons." I grabbed his face and forced him to look me in the eye. "Shacago, are you marrying Zarielle because you love her or because of everything we said to each other on Sunday?"

"I don't think that's any of your business because you already made it real clear that we ain't nothing but co-parents and business partners. Why come to me now acting like you give a fuck? You haven't for the past seven years. You know who did, though? The woman I'm marrying tomorrow evening."

"Shacago, I know I may not always act like it, but I'm down for you more than you'll ever know. Trust me when I say that I care about you and want more for you than you probably want for yourself. All I'm asking is if you're getting married for all the right reasons."

"They're the right reasons to me," he replied, his eyes unblinking. "You moved on. Yet, you acting like I'm supposed to sit here stuck on you while you're out spending time with Marquise. I deserve for a woman to be in my corner, Rosé. Are you willing to be that woman?" I dropped my hands and looked away. "That's what the fuck I thought."

"Shacago—"

"Save it, Rosé. I'm done playing these games. The only person that wins is you. See you tomorrow at the wedding."

I held on to the balcony railing and closed my eyes, doing my best to keep the tears at bay. Everyone was so convinced that Shacago and I were meant to be together, they hadn't taken into account that we might've grown so far apart that there's no coming back from the pain we've caused each other. There was something about the safety Marquise provided that made me believe the best thing I could do for Shacago was to let him go.

CHAPTER 7

The Matrimony

Shacago

"*M*an, where you going?" Xavier asked from underneath the mound of strippers covering him. "The party ain't over until you laid out. This is your last night of freedom—you need to be enjoying it inside of some pussy."

"Nah, I think I'mma go for a walk," I said, finishing off my bottle of champagne and grabbing a brand-new bottle of Hennessey Pure White sitting on a table. "I'll be back in a few."

"You want one of these honeys to go with you?" Xavier replied, motioning to the multiple options sitting on his lap and hovering over him. "I already asked and they down for whatever."

"I'm good, X. Hold that down for me while I'm gone."

I wasted no time popping the bottle of Hennessey and taking it to the head. I was walking with no destination in mind, but I managed to end up on the other side of the resort where the pools were. A real cute honey with a fat ass was pacing back and forth as she argued on the phone in a hushed voice.

"I do a lot for you and it's never enough. I am sick and tired of you always treating me like a piece of shit. You keep making these weak ass excuses and then expect me to be good when they fall through." She turned around and I found myself face-to-face with Parai, who had tears streaming down her cheeks. "I'll talk to you later."

"I see I'm not the only one having relationship troubles," I slurred, pushing her playfully on the shoulder only to send her staggering back a few steps. I grabbed her waist to keep her from falling over. "I'm sorry about that."

Parai pressed herself into me ever so slightly and replied, "It's cool. Don't worry about it."

"Trouble with your man?" I asked, unashamed of my nosiness. "Nigga sound like he taking you for granted."

"He always is. I'm always giving and sacrificing for him, yet he can't do the same. Lately, we keep having the same argument and all he keeps hitting me with is the same 'I love you, baby' line. Love isn't always enough."

I took another swig of liquor. "Facts."

"What are you doing down here? You got a popping ass bachelor party going on upstairs."

"Rosé came up in there asking me all these questions and ruined my whole entire mood. Can we talk about this in your room? You ain't gotta worry about Raven 'cause she with Rosé and Candice."

"Of course," Parai replied, taking in my disheveled appearance and deciding that I needed someone to talk to.

The walk there was silent, with our shoulders brushing ever so slightly since my drunk ass couldn't walk a straight line. Parai laughed the entire time, shaking her head as she let us into the hotel room. I made a beeline for the first double bed and got comfortable, kicking off my shoes, and laying back.

"How do you know that isn't Raven's bed?" Parai asked with her hands on her hips, an amused smile creeping up her face.

"Because a woman like you comes second to no one," I said without hesitation.

Parai plopped down on the edge and replied, "That's what you think."

"That's what I know. I've been in Deuce's club plenty of times and never got a dance from any one of them tired ass strippers."

"You didn't get one from me either."

"I didn't, but you caught my eye and that isn't an easy thing to do. You're always spitting some knowledge to me so let me do the same." I felt my heart racing as she crawled to where I was laying and snuggled up into the crook of my arm. "I don't know who this nigga is, but he's sleeping on your worth. A woman like you isn't one that you get and mistreat. You're beautiful, intelligent, perceptive, and any man that can't see your value is one you don't need in your life."

"I think he knows my value but—"

"There are no 'but's.'" I placed my hand on her lips, noticing they were as soft as they looked. "If a man really loves his woman, she'll never have to question where they stand."

Parai closed her eyes and a single tear rolled down her cheeks. I don't know if it was the Henny or Rosé, but I leaned in and wiped it with my lips. At first, the kiss took Parai by surprise, her eyes widened and she stared at me uncertainly. After noticing how right it felt, she leaned in and closed the distance between us. Kissing Parai felt like an outer body experience, the connection between us so deep that it couldn't even compare to the greatest of highs. Everywhere she touched me—my cheeks, neck, and the way she rubbed my arms—numbed instantly. I tossed aside the bottle in my hand and replaced it with her waist as I sat her on top of me.

"Are you sure about this?" she whispered against my lips.

I whispered into her ear, "I might regret it tomorrow, but I won't regret it tonight."

I pulled Parai out of her sundress and placed one of her delicate nipples into my mouth, swirling and sucking on it. Parai squirmed in my grip, moaning as she gyrated against my already swelling dick. I wanted her bad, but I wanted to savor the moment. Her eyes lit up in surprise as I slid down the bed until I was directly underneath her swollen, wet pussy. I slid her lace cheeky panties to the side and replaced them with my tongue. She tasted sweet, like fresh strawberries, quenching the hunger I felt in the pit of my stomach from the first time I wanted to kiss her.

"Shacago," Parai said as she moaned, riding my face as I tongue fucked her mercilessly, sucking on her clit until she came. Once wasn't enough and I could feel another orgasm coming and sucked up every single last bit of her juices. "You're gonna kill me."

I flipped her onto her back and with a quick toss of my pants, entered her, stretching her walls with each stroke. She met me with each stroke, our motions mirroring each other and growing faster.

"Whose pussy is this?" I demanded, flipping her over and entering her with a sense of urgency.

Parai arched her back and bit her lip as I smacked her on the ass. "It's yours, Shacago!"

As soon as she spoke those words I came, filling her with part of me that I had only shared with a few. It should've felt wrong, but lying next to Parai and kissing her aching lips made everything feel right.

******

"This can't be really happening."

My eyes snapped open and there stood Raven at the foot of the bed, her arms crossed and her brows raised in disbelief. Parai snuggled into me and continued sleeping. I wasn't surprised; I had kept her up all night and we hadn't fallen asleep until only a couple hours ago. It was a night I would remember for a long time because judging by the look on Raven's face she wasn't going to let me forget anytime soon.

"Raven—"

"You're supposed to be getting married today."

"I know I just—"

"Everyone is looking for you all over the place, including, Zarielle, your fiancé."

"Raven, you don't understand."

Raven pinched the bridge of her nose. "I think I understand really well—you dragged us all the way to another country for a last-minute wedding to a woman you don't want to marry. While here, you fucked our receptionist and you're not looking the least bit sorry about it because you're not, are you? Are you?!"

Parai jolted awake and mumbled, "What's going on?"

"You tell me," Raven shot back. "You were all for getting Shacago and Rosé back together. What happened? The dick was too good to pass up?"

I wrapped a sheet around me and approached Raven, who was growing incensed by our nonchalance. "Raven, don't take this out on her."

"I'll take this out on whoever I want because now I have to look my friend in the face and try to break this news to her."

"Raven, please don't tell Rosé about this. We're on bad enough terms as it is, this'll make things worse."

Raven stomped her foot and screwed her face up. "You want me to lie to her?"

"It's not lying if you don't say anything."

"It's a lie by omission."

I let out a sigh, regretting how lax I had been about last night. I opened my mouth to tell her that this technically wasn't any of Rosé's business when Parai cut in and said, "It was a one night thing, Raven. There's no need for anyone to find out about this because it won't happen again. Right, Shacago?"

The tone was subtle, but I could hear the lie in Parai's voice and didn't miss a beat. "Rosé fucked me up last night and all this wasn't nothing but an accident. Can we keep this between us at least for right now?"

Raven grinded her jaw and said, "Shacago, you better fix this and fix it soon. Now put on some clothes and pretend to have woken up on the other side of the beach or something…." She scoffed when I stood there, waiting for her to leave. "Oh, you think you about to stay in here and talk to her? Get in the bathroom and think about what you've done."

I trudged to the bathroom, thinking about how I didn't feel the least amount of guilt about cheating on Zarielle. She had been nothing but good to me and here I was numb to the fact that I cheated on her hours before our wedding. I dressed slowly as I tried to figure out if I should even walk down the aisle.

"Fuck!" I shouted in aggravation as I plopped down on the toilet seat.

Zarielle didn't deserve any of this, but what she really didn't deserve was to be brought to another country and made a fool of in front of our friends and family. What I felt with Parai hadn't worn off and felt like one of the realest relationships I'd experienced in a long time. I knew exactly what I had to do and it would hurt me because once again, I was giving up my happiness for loyalty.

There was a knock on the door and Parai poked her head in. "I got Raven to step out for a few so you don't have to worry—"

"Parai, can I talk to you for a minute?"

She slid in and said, "You're wondering whether or not you should get married today. This wasn't a mistake, but we both know it shouldn't happen again. You've got Zarielle and I have…other stuff happening on my plate."

"So, we good?"

Parai pulled me in for a lingering kiss. "We're more than good. So, go and get married."

Walking back to my room, I thought about Parai and the endless possibilities we could've had. I stopped in my tracks and glanced back at the elevator as I tried to figure out whether or not I had made the best decision for me. I was about to walk back to the elevator when I heard a familiar voice.

"Nigga, where you been?" Xavier said, wrapping an arm around my shoulder and dragging me down the hall. "I have been trying to distract everyone from your disappearance since last night. Where was you at? Found you one of them fine ass honeys walking around here, didn't you?"

"Nah, I passed out on the beach and the hotel staff woke me up."

X stopped walking. "You passed out and put your shirt on inside out? You smell like Dolce & Gabbana, too, and the only person I know who was wearing that was the fine honey you got working the front desk at the shop." I scratched the back of my head, which made him crack up. "You got yourself a side chick the night before your wedding? My nigga!"

"It ain't nothing to celebrate," I said, ignoring the dap he had held out. "It was a one night thing and ain't happening again, aight?"

"That's what you say now, but I'll get the details from you later. We gotta get you ready to say 'I do.' You not having cold feet, right?"

I glanced back to the elevator and back at my brother, who was kind of excited for the festivities. "Nah, fam, I'm good."

Rosé

"You still sitting here looking all depressed?" Candice stood in the doorway of our room, watching as I stared at myself in the mirror. Not a hair was out of place and my makeup was perfect—I even loved how my lilac Marc Jacobs dress fit like a glove.

I pushed myself away from the table and stood up. "I'm not depressed I just feel like—"

"Shacago is making the biggest mistake of his life? Don't worry—this ain't the first time and it won't be the last. Let's just get down there and sit through this wedding because I heard the food afterwards is gonna be bomb."

Candice and Raven had been keeping me occupied since we left the bachelor party. We went back to our room and spent the entire night watching movies and ordering room service (on Shacago's dime since he wanted to be a big baller). It was all good until no one could find him. Cago started worrying and all that did was make me worry, too. I let out a breath I didn't even realize I was holding in when Raven told me that she found him. Shacago and I weren't on good terms right now, but if something happened to him then I don't know what I would—

"Girl, are you gonna stand there and daydream or come and take a seat?" Candice said, motioning to the beautiful beach wedding in front of us.

Twenty white chairs were set out in white sand facing a white arch covered in wild flowers. Shacago and Xavier stood at the podium in deep conversation, Shacago's brows furrowed as he listened to his brother. He looked away from him and our eyes locked, causing my heart to pound. I waved and he inclined his head before returning his attention to Xavier.

"Candice, I can't let him do this," I whispered, tugging her into our seats.

Candice scoffed. "So, you plan on getting back with him?"

"No," I said, shaking my head, "but just because I don't plan on getting back with him doesn't mean that he has to do this. He's settling like he always does. There's someone out there that can make him happy even if it isn't me."

"Girl, I hope you know what you're doing. Because it sounds like you're about to break something that isn't broken. So you don't like Zarielle—nobody likes that bitch. However, that doesn't take away from whatever it is that Shacago sees in her. I was all for you tearing this wedding up when I thought y'all were gonna give it a try, but now? You're stepping out of your lane."

I sunk into my chair. "You're right. I don't know what I was thinking."

"Yup, because if you messed up this wedding you would've blocked the blessing coming your way."

"What?"

A pair of strong arms draped in expensive blue linen wrapped around me and a pair of very familiar lips kissed my cheek. "I know you were supposed to be gone for the weekend, but I couldn't stop thinking about you," Marquise whispered in my ear.

"I can't believe you flew all the way here to spend a night with me," I replied, in awe of his devotion to our relationship. "I was coming back tomorrow morning."

"That was too far," he proclaimed, taking a seat next to me and taking me into his arms. "I called Shacago and asked him if they could spare the seat and he did without a problem. I know the two of you be having ups and downs, but he cares about you. 'Cause no nigga would allow this unless they wanted to see their child's mother happy."

I looked back at the archway and Shacago was staring at me again this time with a hint of a smile. "Thank you," I mouthed, nudging my head towards Marquise, who was now chatting with Candice.

"You're welcome," he mouthed back.

Candice was right: instead of trying to tell Shacago what to do, I needed to be happy for him. I leaned into Marquise and watched with a smile as Shacago made one of the biggest mistakes of his life. It wasn't mine to live, but I would stand in his corner like a real friend should.

CHAPTER 8

Lover's Lane

Shacago

"*L*ook who's back from their honeymoon," Suede shouted from behind the receptionist's desk as I completed my failed attempt to sneak into the shop without being noticed. "How was the Bahamas?"

After our crew celebrated our wedding weekend with us, Zarielle and I hopped on a plane to the Bahamas where we celebrated our honeymoon, courtesy of Deuce, who was happy with the numbers I was pulling in. The five-star resort we stayed at was beautiful and so romantic that if Zarielle wasn't pregnant already, she would've been traveling to the States with my seed. Everything was perfect and I put the fiasco from my bachelor party behind me, vowing to make sure it never happened again.

"It was exactly what I needed after everything that happened two weeks ago. I've moved on from it and I feel like I've restarted."

"That's wassup," Suede replied, dapping me as he went back to working on the sketch pad he had sitting on the desk. "Well, Rosé's been holding it down and got some big names coming down here to get tatted. One of them saw my realism work and requested me, so I'm sitting here practicing."

"Where is Rosé?"

"She's back there on the phone getting in touch with the landlord. The air conditioner's acting up."

I glanced around the lobby and scanned the browsers until I laid eyes on a familiar face. Parai, dressed in a skin tight floral tube dress with her hair hanging around her face in a halo of curls, was showing my portfolio to a couple. She winked and I felt my heart skip a beat. I was hoping no one noticed, but Suede was watching me with a knowing grin on his face when I turned back to him.

"Lemme find out you smashing. She is your type," Suede replied matter-of-factly.

"What type is that?"

Suede looked Parai up and down and said, "If I have to point it out, then I'm only insulting my own intelligence."

"Nigga, get back to work," I said, waving off his assumptions and making my way down the hall to my office.

I entered and found Rosé pacing back and forth, her Yves Saint Laurent pumps damn near wearing a hole into the floor. Whoever she was on the phone with must've been giving her the business because she was red and her eyes were so narrowed that they almost crossed.

"You need to be making your way to my shop now. The central air just cut off and I'm not about to have my clients sweating while they're being tattooed. Do you have any idea how disgusting that is?" Rosé stopped pacing at the sight of me standing there. "If you want your rent money then you'll have somebody here within the next hour...Keep thinking it's a game until you end up in court with your feelings hurt."

"Look at you handling business like a real G," I said once Rosé hung up and took a seat at the edge of my desk. "I heard you been bringing some serious money in here, too. Who you got coming in this week?"

"Some of Marquise's friends are looking to get tatted so I'm booked solid after tomorrow. Which I'm not complaining about because I need to match the cash you put in Cago's college fund," Rosé replied, a smile creeping up her face at the confused expression on mine.

"Come again?"

"Well, it has been a little hard to get Cago enthusiastic about going to school, especially when he sees how successful you've been without college. After Marquise paid for the house, I still had your money and thought about what I could do with it, so I decided to start Cago's college fund. You can imagine how excited he was at seeing that $30,000 invested in his future by his dad. Now he's looking at college catalogs in his spare time."

I plopped down on my chaise, awe knocking the wind out of me. "You did that for me?"

"While you were gone, I've had some time to think about everything that happened at the barbecue. One minute I was preaching to you about how I didn't need a fancy house or car, and the next I was accepting both from my boyfriend. It was hypocritical as fuck and I knew that if I was going to apologize for springing it on you like that, then I had to show you how much I meant it. I decided there was no better way to make it up to you than to give you part of something that no other man would be able to: a vital part of our child's future.

"Do you accept my apology?" Rosé asked, her expression unsure.

As far as I was concerned, everything that happened before the wedding was a thing of the past and we were starting over. I hugged Rosé tight, grateful for her thoughtful gesture. Ever since Cago came into my life, all I wanted was to be everything for him that my father wasn't for me. Being the one to officially jumpstart his education had me walking on cloud nine. Rosé smiled up at me, and back was the woman I once wanted to spend the rest of my life with. The chances of that happening were slim, but it didn't stop me from wanting to lean in and—

"SO, YOU THOUGHT YOU WAS GONNA GET AWAY WITH TRYNA FUCK MY MAN, BITCH!"

Rosé and I flipped over my tattooing chair, hitting the floor in a tangled heap as Yandi leapt on top of us and began raining down blows on a stunned Rosé. It only took two swings for Rosé to start blocking Yandi's punches and landing a few of her own. I tried my best to insert myself between the two women, but shit was getting far too real. Rosé untangled herself from me and had a handful of Yandi's hair wrapped around her fist as she laid into her. Suede appeared out of thin air, grabbing Yandi around the waist and attempting to pull her away from Rosé, who was doing damage with each passing second. I grabbed ahold of Rosé and started pulling her.

"Rosé, let go of her hair," I urged as Suede tried his best to hold a kicking and screaming Yandi.

Rosé let go of Yandi's hair, but not before giving her a departing kick to the face. "That's for coming in my place of business and acting a fucking fool. WHAT THE HELL IS WRONG WITH YOU!"

"Deadass, Rosé?" Yandi spat, shrugging out of Suede's grip and fixing her hair. "Quan told me about how you hit on him when he showed up at your place to get Little X. Bitch, you got a whole wealthy ass boyfriend and you gotta come for what's mines? Why, 'cause he ain't never been feeling you since he first met you?"

"Are you serious right now? Ain't nobody checking for your weak ass boyfriend, Yandi. He came to MY house and started flirting with ME. But your dumbass is too blind to see the obvious because this is the first nigga to pay you some attention since Xavier," Rosé said, her chest heaving as she took a seat on the corner of my desk. "I have fucked with nothing but the biggest and baddest to run these streets. What would make you think I would downgrade?"

"Downgrade?" Yandi said with a bark of laughter as she backed up towards the doorway. "You have no idea what you're talking about because Quan is coming for all these Brooklyn niggas. He'll be running shit sooner than you expect and that's when all the niggas that been hating on him will learn. Trust and believe."

"You sounding real stupid, Yandi," I interjected. "Like you over there getting high with them niggas or something. I don't know whether or not they sent you as a messenger or just for laughs, but let me make myself real clear: if I ever catch you near my shop ever again, I'mma show you who the fuck is running Brooklyn. Now go carry that message to them young niggas."

Yandi ignored me, instead turning her attention to Rosé and saying, "I'mma catch you again, bitch!"

"And get these hands one more time," Rosé promised, flipping her the bird. "Somebody get her the fuck out of here before I forget that we share blood and handle her like I used to do the bitches that would beat her ass back in the day."

Suede closed the door behind them, leaving Rosé and I standing there, chests heaving. Rosé threw herself onto the chaise and screamed into the cushions, pounding her fists until she'd had enough. Sitting up slowly, she laid her head on the armrest and peered up at me through her tousled hair.

"If it ain't one thing with this nigga, then it's another," Rosé said, biting her bottom lip and clenching her fists like she was ready to do some damage. "He needs to be humbled—immediately."

"Niggas like that got a way of pulling the trigger to the gun they placed to their own head. Don't even worry about his corny ass. X and I will handle it."

Rosé and I might always have our ups and downs, but what I won't tolerate is anyone placing her wellbeing at risk. What if Yandi had popped off while Cago was here? Nah, I had plans to nip this in the bud, ASAP.

Xavier

"You was fucking my brother while you was on your honeymoon, wasn't you?" I asked Zarielle as I slipped behind her and placed my hands on her stomach. "I'mma let that shit slide this one time because of the circumstances, but from here on out you better not be having that nigga fuck you with my seed in your stomach, understand?"

Zarielle, who had been quiet and withdrawn since arriving back home last night, leaned into me and said, "Yes, daddy."

"Now how about you relax and let daddy show you how much he's been missing you."

My hands slid up the silk nightgown she was wearing, my dick jumping when I discovered that she didn't have on any panties. I trailed kisses softly down her neck, topping each one with a gentle blow that had her clenching my hand between her legs. I teased her clit the best I could, making small circles. She shouldn't have let out that strangled moan because all it did was excite my hand, which had a mind of its own as it cupped her soaking wet pussy and stroked it. I spread her legs and bent her over the kitchen counter, laughing at the trembles that coursed through her body.

"Did you miss daddy's dick?" I whispered into her ear as my dick stretched her walls. I hit her with two long strokes and wrapped my free hand around her hair, pulling until her ear was next to my lips. "ANSWER ME!"

"Yes, Daddy," Zarielle groaned, backing her ass up and meeting me stroke for stroke. "I missed this dick. Fuck me harder!"

I picked her legs up, wrapping them around my waist and digging into her guts as she slid up the counter and did her best to hold on. It was all in vain because I flipped her ass over and finished handling my business. I broke the straps on her nightgown, allowing her breasts to spill out into my hands. Her back arched and I found myself lost deep inside of—

"Xavier," Zarielle hissed, grabbing my arms and staring up at me with a panicked expression. "The door."

I stopped pumping and that's when I heard it—the rattling of keys and Shacago on the phone with someone. Shit, I had always been so comfortable with the thrill of fucking Zarielle and Shacago possibly walking in, but this shit was a whole new ball game. With Quan all in my pockets, I had too much to lose and right now that little nigga was the least of my fears. My legs were shaking as I stood there stupidly waiting to get caught 'cause whether or not Zarielle and I straightened up it was smelling like sex all in the air. The door opened and I heard Shacago take one step before the most miraculous thing happened.

"Damn, I forgot to pick up Zarielle's prenatal vitamins from the pharmacy. Lemme back up out the apartment before she hears my ass and has a titty attack..."

The door quietly shut and the lock clicked in place. I didn't move until I heard Shacago's voice fade as he traveled down the hall, laughing with whoever he was on the phone with. Zarielle pulled her torn nightgown to her chest and climbed clumsily off the counter, running down the hall to her bedroom while I stood there with a limp dick and a mess to clean up. Pulling the container of Clorox wipes from the bottom cabinet, I knew this was only the first of more to come.

******

I can't call it nothing less of a miracle that not only did Shacago show up an hour later, but he brought lunch with him. After we were almost caught fucking on the counter, Zarielle had locked herself in her bedroom, ignoring my knocks and demands that she open the door. I don't know if it's the pregnancy hormones or her being married, but she better get her shit together real quick and remember that Shacago can't protect her all the time. She was lucky that eating some banging ass soul food from Claretha's, a local spot down the block, had me in a better mood than I was in twenty minutes ago.

"What's going on, fam?" I said, wolfing down the plate of fried chicken, baked macaroni and cheese with collard greens. "You came in looking stressed as fuck."

"Your baby moms and that young nigga she been fucking with are what's bothering me. You know she came to the shop and fought Rosé over him?"

I let out a bark of laughter and damn near choked. "What the fuck she think that little punk was gon' do with a grown ass woman like Rosé? I don't like her being that nigga, but I might have to keep Little X at Mom's house 'cause Quan obviously got her lost and turned out."

"I'm thinking about handling him over the weekend. I was on the phone with some of my hittas and we working on riding out this weekend. You down?" Shacago asked, his eyes never leaving mine as he took a gulp of beer.

I suppressed an internal sigh, knowing that fucking with a cocky muthafucker like Quan, it was only a matter of time something like this might happen. Was I against Shacago putting a bullet in this nigga's head? No, only 'cause I wanted to be the one to do it. The only factor that kept me from riding with this plan was that I had no idea whether or not someone would expose my secret if he was killed. As far as I was concerned, Quan had to live for now.

"Nigga, do you know how suspect that's gon' look?" I said, my mind working overtime to think of a really good reason for why Shacago couldn't make my dreams come true. "Yandi shows up to your shop fighting over him and days later he disappears? Niggas already say you be all up Rosé ass, do you really want them thinking you go that hard over your baby moms?"

"Who said I be all up Rosé's ass?" Shacago countered, making it clear that all he heard was "Rosé" and "ass."

I sunk into my seat, shaking my head at this oblivious fool. "You had a whole entire bitch fit when her man bought her a house. Now Quan is saying that she tryna smash him when we know he ain't up to par? I'm positive it will be known that you got a soft spot for another woman that isn't your wife. Speaking of your wife, how are you gon' break the news to Zarielle that you plan on killing her cousin?"

"That ain't for her to know."

"She'll put two and two together once she hears about Rosé."

"That ain't why I'm ending that nigga."

"Like I said, that's how it's gon' look," I said with a shrug of my shoulders. "But if that's what you wanna do, then you know I'mma ride out regardless."

Shacago took his time cutting up a piece of baked macaroni and replied, "You sure about that? Or you just gon' keep avoiding Quan 'cause he holding something over your head?"

"Excuse me?"

"X, you don't ever back down from shit, but Quan brings out a pussy side of you that I ain't never seen before. So, you plan on telling me why or should I go and ask him?"

For the second time today, I was humbled. I kept thinking Shacago could be plied with my logic and never notice its inconsistencies. Sometimes I kept forgetting that although I'm the smarter brother, he's smart himself.

Smart enough to piece together everything perfectly.

"I'ont know what you—"

"Man, cut that lying shit out," Shacago said, pushing away from the table. "He fucked you up, didn't he? Him and all them niggas that showed up at Rosé's housewarming?"

Any hotter and I was gon' find myself in hell sooner than I expected. When nonchalance didn't work, anger always came through. "You bugging right now, Shacago. I don't back down from no-motherfucking-body, you hear me? I ain't going after Quan 'cause I don't wanna look like you: a nigga that ain't over his baby moms!"

"Keep telling yourself that," Shacago said with a curt nod. "I only hope for your sake that you don't tell me what the fuck is really going on when the lil' bitch has you stuck in a situation you can't get yourself out of."

"Man, fuck outta here," I shot back as I thought about that situation becoming my reality. "I'm tryna look out for you. A simple nigga like Quan is already waiting for you to attack him—he's anticipating it happening sooner rather than later. You gotta wait him out…let him get comfortable. Then you strike and rip his shit up from the inside out."

I could tell that Shacago wanted to press even more, but there was no way in hell I was going to admit to anything. He opted for the smarter route and replied, "You're absolutely right, X. I'm glad I can always count on you to keep me level headed. I'm sorry for pressing you, bro, but I don't like the idea of you walking around with a target on your back."

Staring into Shacago's eyes, for the first time in my life, I couldn't read him. I felt chills creep up the back of my neck and was relieved for a reason to look away. My phone lit up with an SOS message from Deuce, who I had been improving my relations with. He was pleased with the way I handled business while Shacago was out of town and it was only a matter of time that I got the promotion I deserved.

"Deuce hit you up, too?" Shacago said, turning his attention from me to his buzzing phone. "And he did it with a text? Lemme find out this old nigga moving into the 21st Century."

******

Tasty was popping when we arrived, with the ballers going harder than usual. The girls were having a mighty fine time—they looked like they were on cloud nine as money literally rained from the VIP section above. Shacago and I looked up to see who was up there making it rain, but only managed to make out a few shadows.

"Shit, what's the celebration for?" Shacago asked no one in particular.

You could only imagine our surprise when one of the bottle girls walking by and replied, "We're now under new management."

"New management?" I echoed as we cut through the crowded club. "You think this nigga, Deuce, is about to skip town or something? I can't think of another reason why he would sell the club."

"Well if he is, I hope he plans on putting us on notice. I paid my debt to society once and I ain't about to do that shit again," Shacago replied, fixing himself before we climbed the stairs to Deuce's office.

I knocked on his office door with the pattern he taught all of us and waited before drumming it out again. There wasn't an answer. Shacago and I exchanged glances before I tried again, this time louder. It was unusual for Deuce to leave his office unattended. Even if he wasn't present, someone else always is, making sure the money comes straight up from the floor without any problems.

"This was a setup," Shacago said, pulling out his piece and nudging his head towards the door. "Open it up and move out the way."

I pulled out my own piece and did as I was told, backing up so Shacago could enter while I brought up the rear. The office was dark save for someone sitting behind the desk with their hands folded.

"Deuce, what the fuck you sitting in the dark for?" I asked, flipping the lights to find myself in the middle of a massacre.

The same men that had beat me black and blue lay on the floor looking like chopped meat. They were all bent at awkward angles as their eyes stared vacantly ahead, probably surprised at how painful an ass whupping could be. Blood oozed from the machete slices and gunshot wounds riddling their bodies, coloring the white shag carpet a deep crimson.

"I always thought these walls could use better artwork than all these Hustler posters," I said, referring to the blood splattering the walls. My eyes finally traveled to the desk where an extremely rigid Deuce sat. "Oh shit, they got this nigga Deuce. How? Who?"

"I'm guessing we're supposed to read that and find out," Shacago said, pointing to the white piece of paper propped up next to Deuce's hands.

Shacago approached the desk where Deuce's body sat propped up like an awkward marionette doll. His neck was sliced clean open and I know he wished he would've known he was dying tonight so he could wear anything other than the snow-white suit he was dressed in. Now he was looking like a throwback Popsicle.

"It says for us to come upstairs to the VIP section," Shacago said, ushering me out the office and wiping off any trace evidence of us being there. "Who the fuck you think is up there? I heard from the streets that Pretty Johnny and Deuce been beefing over some territory borders."

"Pretty Johnny know better than to come up in here on some bullshit. Plus, they'd never meet here at the club. This is a sacred space for Deuce. Whoever came here and did this was going for the jugular.

Straight savage."

Neptune, the bouncer for the VIP section, gave us a once over before allowing us through. When you been in the game, nothing surprises you anymore, but when I saw Quan sitting on Deuce's white leather sofa smoking a blunt with his two favorite girls, I knew I had to be dreaming. This shit can't be real. Someone had to just be making this shit up and writing one of the worse books ever.

"Bonjour, niggas," Quan said, passing the blunt to Sprinkles, who took a pull and winked at me. "Surprised to see me?"

Chairs were placed behind our kneecaps, forcing us to sit down. I was secretly grateful for the gesture because my legs were shaking so bad I was damn near knock-kneed. Shacago was the picture of calm with his gun hanging lazily from his fingers. I could tell Quan wanted to flex some of his newfound power but decided against it to keep from looking childish.

"I always knew somebody would knock off that nigga, Deuce. I didn't expect it to be a little kid playing with his daddy's gun," Shacago said without preamble. "I hope you got a plan, lil' nigga, 'cause you're about to find yourself answering to the big dogs. Caesar and them don't take too kindly to their employees being replaced without their explicit permission."

"Who says I ain't talked to Caesar?" Quan countered, accepting the blunt and taking a long pull. He blew the smoke into our faces and I had to keep from bodying this bitch. "When you about to take over some new territory it only makes sense to get in contact with the distributors. This might surprise you, but I had Caesar's blessing.

Deuce was becoming a liability with the way the Feds were looking at him. I was promised this spot so long as I handled him."

"Aren't you quite the opportunist," I said, my lip curled with contempt. "What you tryna say, we work for you now?"

"That's not what I'm tryna say—that's what I'm telling you." Quan momentarily disappeared behind the cloud of smoke and when he returned he was wearing a sinister smile. "A lot of changes are about to start coming y'all way and I can promise that you won't like any of them."

Looking at this smug motherfucker, I knew he had to be stopped. Glancing at Shacago, I took a deep breath and swallowed my pride because as of right now it wasn't getting me anywhere. I would have to do the one thing I hated to. Tell the truth.

Eventually.

"Can you fucking believe this shit?" Shacago said as we left out the club after receiving a heads up from Quan to look out for his call about our next shipment. "I know you said that we need to wait but—"

"Fuck all that shit I said earlier," I said, sliding into the passenger seat and staring straight ahead. "We taking this nigga out and that's word on everything I love. Don't worry about shit—I got it under control."

"This is sounding real personal," Shacago said with a smirk.

I patted my piece and gave a noncommittal shrug. "Something like that."

CHAPTER 9

The Re-Up

Rosé

*Y*andi may have fucked up my mood for the morning, but once noon hit and my first client walked through the door, money was on my mind. Keeping it cute and classy was as well because my client was Khalise Andraya, an Instamodel, that had the potential to have people showing up to the shop in droves. Staying on the arm of every rap superstar gained her well over five million followers and Rosé's Tattoo Shop needed that exposure. The orchids I tatted along her ribcage were some of my best work, and I had Yandi and her hate to thank for that. As much as I wanted to head home and talk about it with Candice and Raven, there was one person that I needed to run this by for their opinion.

"Hey, Rosé," Tracey said, opening the door wider for me to step into the house. "It's good to see you…here…at the house."

I shot her a look and asked, "Am I supposed to be somewhere

else, Tracey?"

"Yeah—at your house. That's where Elijah said he was heading to have dinner and help you set up your entertainment center…." Tracey trailed off as her expression became cold. "You haven't heard from him all day, have you?"

"I…uh—"

"No need to answer that," Tracey replied coolly, motioning for me to follow her to the kitchen. "The last thing I want is to put you in an awkward position. I ordered some takeout since Elijah wasn't coming home until late. Again. Would you like some Chinese?"

"No, I…uh…have dinner plans with my boyfriend tonight," I said, grimacing when I saw how jerky Tracey's motions became as she made herself a plate of fried rice and spare ribs.

"Oh, well if you change your mind then you're more than welcome to make yourself a plate. If you'll excuse me, I have some work that I need to catch up on…."

I watched as she hurried down the hall and upstairs, her shoes nearly stomping a hole in the floor. Spending my entire life being compared to Eli, I was floored at the fact that he was apparently up to no good. Since this was possibly a once in a lifetime moment, I didn't hesitate to call him. It went straight to voicemail.

"Elijah, I'm at your house," was all I said before hanging up.

I held up five fingers and counted slowly, a Kool-Aid smile on my face.

Five.

Four.

Three.

Two—

"What are you doing at my house?" Elijah hissed, making me smile even harder. My brother was squirming and I was about to find out why.

"The better question is why aren't you at your house and using mine as a cover up without tell me?" I whispered, hoping Tracey wasn't at the top of the stairs listening.

Elijah sighed. "Because I was handling some business for work and I didn't want Tracey worrying."

"What kind of business could you have to handle that would make her worry?"

"I'll tell you about it when I get home."

I glanced at my watch not once, not twice, but three times when Elijah walked through the door fifteen minutes later, his shirt wrinkled and his sport coat slung over his shoulder. He saw me taking in his disheveled appearance and held up his hand, silencing me before I could ask some pressing questions. I wasn't sure who he thought I was, but he was about to find out.

"You look like you've been up to no good," I noted, my eyes taking in the rest of his unkempt appearance while he made himself a plate of food. "And you're hungry. What have you been up to?"

Elijah plopped down across from me, stuffing his mouth as he mulled over an answer. He settled with, "I've been doing some work on finding out who killed Angelica and Gabriel. I was meeting with my informant tonight and they don't live in the safest neighborhood."

"Meaning...?"

"I have to remove my shirt when we talk. They're paranoid and keep thinking I have some wires on me."

I cocked an eyebrow at him and replied, "Mmm'kay...."

"Rosé, don't start with that shit. I already have to do damage control because you're doing popups. Now what is it that you came over here to talk about?"

I gave him the rundown about my situation with Yandi, making sure to mention that this all started because of Quan's petty ass. Elijah listened closely, chewing his food slowly as he absorbed every detail. When I was finished, I sat back and waited to hear what his solution was to this problem. In typical Elijah fashion, he had to make it into something it didn't need to be.

"I can build a case on him and have him locked up between six months and a year. I'll need some information on him, though. You plan on helping me out with that?"

My lips tightened and I replied coldly, "No, I'm not helping you send anyone else to jail."

"So, then you need to mind your business and let that girl ruin her own life. I know she's your favorite cousin and everything, but sometimes you have to learn how to distance yourself from people who aren't headed towards the same goal you are."

I sat back in my seat, crossing my arms, and shrugging off my brother's complacency. "What if something happens to her, Eli? Will you be able to live with yourself knowing you could've done something to prevent it?"

"Yes," Elijah replied without hesitation. "Yandi is a grown ass woman and if she thinks her entire life is supposed to be dope boys and designer clothes, then who am I to get in the way of that? The price of the lifestyle is paid for in blood. I know that, you know that, and Yandi does as well. So, unless you're here with some information that might help me find whoever is killing off employees at the shop—"

Here we go, I thought as I climbed out of my chair and headed for the door. Sometimes I forgot that if it didn't have anything to do with locking black men up for the rest of their lives, Elijah wasn't trying to hear shit.

******

My bad mood didn't improve on my way home. The old Rosé would've pulled out a blunt and smoked it all the way home so she could be in a good mood to see Cago. Unfortunately, the new Rosé was recognized damn near everywhere she went and the last thing she wanted was to be seen all over the Internet blazing up. I was still huffing and puffing when I reached my door. A pair of white roses set in front of my apartment door decorated in rose gold foil.

"Aww, my man is so sweet," I gushed, entering the apartment to find Candice sitting in the living room watching TV, a slumbering Cago in her lap.

Candice took one look at the bouquet in my hand and brought her nosy ass over to get a look at the card poking out the top. "Who are those from?" she asked, dancing on her tiptoes.

"Who else would they be from? Marquise, duh," I replied, opening the envelope and looking at the poem written in red ink:

Roses are red,

Violets are blue,

One look at that smile of yours

Reminds me of how much I'm missing you.

Candice eyed the poem wearily. "That don't sound like something Marquise would write. I also don't see him leaving it at your doorstep and not knocking to come in. Girl, either you got a secret admirer or a stalker, and I suggest you find out before you get any more creepy gifts, like a vial of blood or lock of your hair sheddings…"

"I know who this is from. Quan. His bitch ass showed up here flirting the other day and now he's sending me flowers? Ugh," I said, tearing up the card and tossing the flowers into the trash.

"Now that we have that mystery solved, you can explain to me where you got that ugly knot from."

For the second time tonight, I told the story of Yandi and Quan as I got ready for my date. When I finished, Candice gave me the same reply that Elijah had except she had a different theory on the entire situation.

"I think you're trying to save Yandi out of guilt for what happened all those years ago with you and Shacago. You couldn't save him, so you're trying to save her. The problem is that she doesn't deserve your good graces for what you did to someone else. You know what you have to do, right?"

I thought about it and she made perfect sense. "Separate them both and tell Shacago the truth? I had a feeling you might say that."

"When do you plan on doing this?"

"Sunday night," I promised. "I'll come clean to him on Sunday night."

Xavier

"X, we been at this for the past three days. Are we handling these niggas or not?" my temporary second in command, Loon, asked as we sat parked outside of Tasty. "Fuck, my girl think I'm out here cheating on her with these strip club hoes 'cause niggas keep saying they see me here."

"What does that have to do with me and how we handle business? If ya bitch can't handle you out here in these streets, then maybe you need to get a job at McDonald's or something. Maybe I need to find a real rider. Do I?"

"Nah, that's not what I was tryna—"

"Then shut the fuck up and keep your eyes on the door," I barked. "Shit, my son could do a better job than your bitch ass."

I was ten minutes into finessing Gabi for some nudes, when Loon tapped me. Quan and his entourage was rolling out without the usual strippers that graced their arms every night. I sent texts to the rest of my team to get ready to follow these niggas. Tonight had to go off without a hitch if I planned on executing Phase 2 with Shacago.

"You sure this is the night? It's Friday and I'm sure they might be headed to another party or something," Loon said as he pulled off and kept a decent distance between us.

"They been in that club for days on end and when Quan ain't there he's usually at Yandi's for the night. But tonight, her salon stays open late, so she ain't gon' be home no time soon. Thursday is the night

130

he'll make his move."

Loon nodded agreeably. "You right about that, fam. He gon' have to make his move when she won't notice. I see they going a different way tonight."

For the past few days, Quan and his boys would head to Yandi's salon, pick her up, drop her and Little X off, chill there for a few hours, and Quan would stay in for the night while his niggas went to handle business. That left turn they typically made was absent, and they kept going straight until they made a left and started heading for Manhattan.

"Of course, he'd keep the rest of his business far away from where he's shitting," I murmured, knowing that the $20,000 I had been giving this nigga was for more than a penthouse like he claimed. "Loon, your girlfriend gon' be happy tonight 'cause you might be able to make it home to her before midnight if things go our way."

"That's if I go home to her," Loon replied, shooting me a nervous grin. "I am fucking one of the strippers at Tasty."

"Deadass?"

We enjoyed the laugh because once we crossed that bridge and made our way to Harlem, it was nothing but business from here on out. Quan and his boys slowed down when they reached some projects on East 143rd Street. Loon parked and we watched as Quan and his crew exited their cars. The niggas posted up in front of the building they entered. We shot them looks of contempt before returning to the conversation at hand.

"How we supposed to know which—"

I silenced Loon with my hand as I rolled down my window

enough to hear the conversation going on across the street.

"...see that nigga every week. Who he going up in there to see, though?" one of the men asked.

"The girl that live in 11G. Nataysia, Kem little sister. Ever since Kem got knocked, that nigga been coming around taking care of her. They be all over 125th shopping. Nigga treat her like a pot of gold. I'm assuming he's Kem peoples."

I rolled my window back up and turned to Loot. "And now we wait."

******

This Nataysia bitch must've had a pussy made out of gold because Quan was up there for three hours. His men made several trips to the supermarket, the corner store, and the soul food spot across the street. I had to give respect where it was due—the nigga may be a scumbag, but at least he knew how to properly take care of his side chick. I was halfway asleep when I heard them coming out of the building.

"They can't do nothing quiet to save their lives, can they?" Loon muttered as we watched them pile into their respective cars and speed off into the night.

I pulled my hood on until it nearly reached my nose. "Don't even stress that shit, fam; that's gon' be their downfall."

The block was deserted when me and a couple of my hittas crossed the street and entered the building. I had Loon waiting with the car running 'cause shit was likely to pop off. We discussed the plan on the elevator ride up, leaving no room for failure because if Quan even got a whiff of what's going on then we'd all be dead.

"Let's do this," I said as the elevator doors opened.

Soca music blasted through the hallways, making our arrival even more stealth-like. I would bet my entire stash that it was coming from the house of the night. As we traveled down the hallway I was proven right—the door of the corner apartment was shaking on its hinges.

Knock! Knock! Knock!

I stood there with my arms crossed in front of me, flexing my newly healed one a couple times to keep it from locking. I knocked three more times and could hear someone yelling for us to wait. The locks clicked and I didn't hesitate to kick the door open when I saw the knob turn. A girl no older than twenty flew into the living room and hit the floor with a thud. We filed in and the door was shut before she could comprehend what was happening. She bolted upright only to be greeted with a kiss from the butt of my gun, knocking her right back on the floor.

"If you feel the need to scream, lemme know so I can give you something to scream for," I said, placing my gun underneath her chin. "Understand?"

She nodded her head ever so slightly. "Yeah."

The music lowered to a decent volume and one of my hittas returned to the living room with some good news. "Ain't nobody else here and it looks like she lives by herself."

"Of course, she does. Quan needs to keep his meal ticket safe from harm, right?" I said, shoving the gun deeper into the girl's throat. "Bring me two chairs and some rope."

"Please, if you want money, I can give you money. I got a whole bunch in the safe back there. You can have as much as you want. Please don't kill me," the girl whimpered, tears streaming down her mocha colored cheeks.

The chairs arrived and I tied her up in one using the plastic shopping bags her groceries arrived in only hours ago. I sat in the other one watching her, taking in the wild look in her eyes and that thick, juicy lip poked out. This was a baby compared to Yandi. If I had something that needed safekeeping, she'd be the last person I'd entrust it too. The pussy was probably good though, and she looked like she minded her business, so I'd probably stash it here without her knowing.

"I don't want any money," I replied with a wave of my hand. "I'm looking for the envelope that Quan gave you to hold for him."

"Envelope? I don't know what you're talking about," she insisted. "Quan comes here to buy me food and clothes because—"

"I ain't come here to find out about the shit he do for you. All I want is the piece of paper and I'll leave you alone."

"I'm telling you that there ain't no paper here."

"What about your bills? Where you keep the envelopes with your bills?"

Nataysia sobbed, her wails almost topping the fast paced Soca beat playing in the background. "Quan takes all the bills with him. I'm telling you he ain't never left no envelope here. If he did, trust me I would give it to you!"

"You mentioned a safe. What's the code?" I demanded, tapping her on the chin.

"Are you gonna let me go if I tell you?"

"You ain't in a position to be trying to bargain. Tell me what the code is before I put a bullet in your head and figure it out myself."

After a few seconds of mental Ping-Pong, she said, "The code is 1-0-2-8."

"Go check the safe and see if he put it in there," I told one of my hittas. While he disappeared to the back, I kept the conversation going. "This is a nice place you got here. Brand new living room set, big ass television, and he feeds you well, too. That's this season's Moschino, ain't it? He keeping you looking real lovely. Giving him that good pussy, huh?"

Nataysia was about to reply when my hitta returned with the verdict. "Ain't nothing in the safe but some jewelry and thirty stacks."

"Pocket it," I commanded, rising from my chair and staring down at Nataysia, who was silently crying as she shook her head. "You sure you ain't seen that envelope?"

"I already told you that I ain't seen no envelope. Where are you going? You're gonna leave me here?" she asked my retreating figure.

I turned back and raised my gun. "You'll have a little something to keep you company."

I pulled the trigger and Nataysia screamed as her head bucked back, the force of it causing her chair to tip over. One of my hittas accepted my gun for disposal as we made our way back downstairs.

"You think that nigga gon' notice something is up when she don't call him?" one of them asked as we boarded the elevator.

I held up the cellphone I had snatched off her and gave it a little wiggle. "I don't think that's a problem we gon' have."

CHAPTER 10

You Give Me Butterflies

Shacago

"*I* can't believe you're about to work for that little fucker," Rosé said disapprovingly, her brow furrowed as she cleaned her equipment. "He killed Deuce? He's a demon and instead of working for him you need to…"

"To what?" I asked Rosé, who had become red and embarrassed as she continued to clean.

"Nothing."

"Rosé, you know how much I hate when people don't finish their thoughts. What you over there boiling about?"

Rosé plopped down into her seat and tossed the paper towels in her hand. "This situation with Yandi. It's been two days and I still haven't heard back from her. I've tried calling her, texting her, and I even called my aunt. I'm guessing that Quan is hitting her off 'cause she usually checks Yandi when she knows she's wrong. Everybody keeps telling me that I need to leave it alone and let her learn herself but—"

"That's your cousin and you don't want to see anything happen to her. You ain't got to defend yourself to me—Xavier is my little brother. If I wouldn't have stepped in to save his hardheaded ass, he'd be dead twenty times over by now. Now what is it that you tryna have done to Quan?"

Rosé placed her head into her hands and sighed. "I want him to go away."

"You just so happen to be in luck because between you and I, that's what me and X been working on for the past couple days. I know we can do it except there's one problem: that lil' nigga always travels with a pack. He's impossible to get alone, and even though we got the numbers, I'm not tryna lose any of my men off of no personal shit."

Rosé glanced at her watch. "If you need anything then don't hesitate to ask. I gotta head out and pick up dinner for Cago and Candice. Shacago?"

"Yes?"

"I'm…uh…having a dinner tomorrow night and I was wondering if you'd wanna stop by. Zarielle is more than welcome," Rosé said, as she packed her purse and slung it over her shoulder. "Can you make it?"

Rosé went from angry to nervous, barely looking at me as she shrugged into her jacket. I wanted to ask her about her sudden change of mood, but figured I would find out tomorrow night. "Sure, we'll be there."

"Cool. I'll see tomorrow night. You got the lockup?"

"Of course," I said, following her out of her station and to the front door to lock it behind her.

Everyone must've called it a night because there wasn't a soul in sight. Knowing my crew, they were out partying with the cache that our shop had received since tatting the baddest in the industry. Rosé gave me a peek at the books and with the numbers everyone was pulling, there was no doubt in my mind that I could step away from the game and start tatting full time.

"You making sure she gets in her car? What a gentleman," a slick voice said behind me.

I had my hand on my waist to grab my piece when her tinkling laughter filled my ears followed by a kiss on the cheek. Parai stood there, bobbing on her heels and wearing a Cheshire cat grin. It was the first time we had been alone since DR and I wasn't sure what my next move should be. I didn't have to worry too much because Parai had a plan of her own. Gone was the bodycon dress she wore earlier—it was now replaced by a black silk robe.

"Everyone packed up and left early tonight, so I was wondering if you could give me one of those famous 'Shacago Stanfield' tattoos you've been promising me," she said before sashaying down the hall to my office.

I promised myself that what happened in DR wouldn't happen again—I was a married man after all—but there was something about that look Parai gave me over her shoulder that had me thinking I was risking it all tonight. *Ain't nothing wrong with tattooing her,* I thought as I closed my office door. *This is for my portfolio.* Parai slipped out of her robe, the silky material caressing her satin skin before hitting the floor. Her naked body was just as flawless as I remembered; my dick agreed, too, as it twitched in my pants.

"I wanted to do something more personal to you. I know it's a little different, but I was thinking about starting with some lavender plants on your back," I said, setting everything up so I could get myself together.

"That sounds perfect. Lavender has multiple meanings. Devotion. Love. Purity. Silence." I became rigid as her arms wrapped around my waist. "I know we said we would remain friends, but I haven't been able to stop thinking about you. I won't tell if you won't."

"I'm married now, Parai. You mean to tell me that you ain't got a problem with fucking a married man?"

Parai and her warmth were gone with those words. I heard her plop down on my chair and sniffle. My intentions weren't to hurt her feelings; I was trying to do the right thing for my wife and myself. Part of me wanted to leave her alone and allow her to get herself together, but I remembered that connection we shared. I took a seat and allowed her to rest her head on my shoulder.

"I didn't mean to upset you," I said, rubbing her thigh consolingly.

She sniffled. "It's not your fault. You said something that I really needed to hear. You ever sometimes feel like you fell in love with the right person at the wrong time?"

I thought about the night Rosé walked back into my life. "I have a time or two."

"I'm stuck in the middle of that and you…you've given me what

I've been looking for and just like with my current situation, I can't have you." She peered up at me, those tears in her eyes caused my heart to break. "Don't give me something beautiful, Shacago. I want something ugly because my heart is breaking."

I wiped the tears from her eyes and said, "I got you."

A cliché move would've been to give Parai that basic ass broken heart with a quote, but she was better than that. I sketched up the image that was plastered to the back of my eyelids. Parai sobbing intensified until the needle punctured her skin; she bit her bottom lip and closed her eyes. I knew that look because I had felt it before.

She was getting high off the pain.

Every swirl was taking her farther away from real life, and every shade was a reminder of how life was never black and white. I took my time, savoring the masterpiece I was creating on her side that flowed into her thigh. The Sunday morning sun was peeking through my blinds as I was layering on the finishing touches to Parai's first of many stories. She was fast asleep when I shook her awake to see the finished product.

"It's…exactly what I needed," Parai said, admiring the self-portrait on her thigh. It was that same vulnerable face she had made when she looked up at me. The tears, that lip, and the heartbreak in her eyes. "I love it. And you put pieces of lavender in my hair…this is everything. You told my story and I can't thank you enough."

I began rubbing it down with A&D and wrapping it up for her to head home. "I couldn't have done it without you being my muse. I've been looking forward to this moment and it was well worth the wait."

We stood there in an awkward silence, unable to find the right words. Our eyes somehow met and that's when every promise I made to myself fell out the window. I leaned in for a kiss and Parai backed away, her expression unsure.

"I've been through this before," Parai said, holding up her hands. "If you can't give me all of you then I need to leave."

"You're right," I said, putting my hands up and hanging my head in shame. "You deserve better and I shouldn't have even tried that with you."

"I'll…uh…get dressed and head out," Parai replied, nearly killing herself to get out of the room.

I banged my head against the wall, shaking it back and forth. Everything was going perfect with Zarielle and me, and here I was contemplating cheating on her. We were having a child. She has been in my corner since day one. I made a vow to spend the rest of my life with her.

"Damn, lemme go and apologize to—"

I opened the door and there she was standing there with that look in her eyes. We crashed into each other, our lips locking and days of built up sexual tension exploding. I carried her to my desk, the same one I christened with my wife, and laid her down like a piece of fine china.

"Parai, I can't—"

Parai silenced me with a kiss. "And I shouldn't, but the connection I feel with you won't allow me to leave you alone. At least you want me and care about me unlike…he's not important. I know you have to go home to her, take care of her, make love to her, and I'm okay with that. I just want the piece of you that you haven't given her yet: your heart."

Under different circumstances, I would've given Parai the world. It became impossible once real life set in, creating obligations and agreements I had to sign in blood. The price of loyalty was loyalty in return and maybe one day my debt to Zarielle would be repaid. But for today, I would make love to Parai under the Sunday morning sun.

Xavier

Quan: Did you finish up your homework like I told you to?

Me: I finished it last night. Now I'm sitting here reading.

Quan: Good. Keep it that way. I told Kem I was gon' make sure you kept up with your schoolwork and that's what I plan on doing. I'll hit you up later.

I stared down at the third message exchange I shared with Quan over the past three days. As it turned out, Nataysia wasn't his side chick like I initially thought—as it turns out she was his nigga's baby sister that he was taking care of while he did a bid. I pried a little to see if he had any intentions of visiting her any time soon and luckily for me, Thursday was their only meet up day. I figured that at least there was an upside to this entire situation. Quan wouldn't have to know that he failed his boy by being too damn arrogant. Then I recalled all the messages he sent to Nataysia and figured I would tell him just to make him sick.

"I'm surprised shorty ain't make it on the news," Loon said as we cruised down the empty Brooklyn streets.

"'Cause they ain't find her body yet, that's why," I reminded him. "Once the news get ahold of something like that, though, it'll be everywhere and you know who the last one to be seen near her? Quan. He'll be long gone 'cause we killed him and then we'll watch the police search all over for him."

"That's mad smart," Loon said, nodding his head vigorously.

"That's why I fuck with you, X. 'Cause you always think of everything."

"Everything except how I'mma get this nigga alone. He always got somebody up under him and ever since he took over Deuce's spot it's only gotten worse."

I was still in deep thought about it when we pulled up to Yandi's shop. It was slow for a Sunday morning, which was exactly what I needed because if his side chick didn't have that envelope then his main would.

"I hope you rolled up in here to make plans to take your son for the weekend," Yandi said from her head stylist seat. She glanced over my shoulder at Loon, who locked the door behind him and took a seat next to it. "What the fuck are you up to, Xavier?"

I noticed that the one hairdresser and her client had become nervous. I let them know that there was no need to worry and asked Yandi politely, "Can I talk to you in your office for a minute?"

"Fine, but it has to be quick because I have a client in twenty minutes. Make sure you open that door for whoever rings the bell, Loon. I can't afford to lose any clients behind y'all bullshit," Yandi said as I followed her down the hall to her office.

Once we were enclosed in the tiny space, my eyes started roving over every piece of paper in sight: the folders in the corner, the big ass file cabinet in the corner of the room, I was even wondering how much paper Yandi had on her desk that she didn't pay attention to.

"You came here to talk to me or go through my stuff? Or did Rosé send you?" Yandi inquired, taking a seat at the edge of her desk.

"I just came to ask about—Rosé? What happened with Rosé?"

"So, get this, Quan goes to pick up Little X and she has the audacity to hit on him. Talking about she's with Marquise because of his money and title, but she wouldn't mind if they did something on the low. Quan wasn't even gonna tell me, but he thought I should know that not everyone you break bread with is looking to eat. Sometimes they're out to covet what's yours. Can you believe that shit?"

Standing there looking at an eager Yandi, a fluorescent light bulb went off in my brain. Of course when we were together I knew she was a ride or die willing to do whatever it took to make sure we stayed winning. Now she was with a bum ass nigga that cared more about an image than business being handled properly, so he made sure to find a bitch he could spoon feed that same mentality. There wasn't nothing real about Yandi 'cause all she did was blindly follow whatever nigga was paying her bills. Everything I taught her was gone and replaced by juvenile bullshit like he-say-she-say.

There was no way in hell Quan would entrust this stupid bitch with anything.

"That's crazy," I lied knowing damn well Rosé wouldn't even let a nigga like Quan wipe her ass with his tongue. "I'm not gon' lie. I did come over here to try and squash that beef with you, but now that I heard your side I guess I'll just mind my business and let shit rock. Also, I was wondering if I could get Little X this weekend. I'm thinking about taking him to a game."

"I'm cool with that. I'll have him packed and ready on Friday," Yandi replied easily.

"Yandi, Erica's here!" someone called from the front.

"I gotta go. Erica's my biggest money maker," Yandi said, brushing past me.

I took a couple steps out of her office and asked, "You mind if I use your bathroom?"

"As long as you don't take a shit," Yandi said, rushing her fast ass down the hall and leaving me standing there.

I closed the bathroom door and snuck back into her office. After riffling through the papers on her desk and the file cabinets, I was positive that Yandi wasn't holding on to any envelope revealing everything. There was only one conclusion I could come up with.

"The nigga played me," I said to Loon once we were in the privacy of the car. "There ain't no stupid ass letter. I checked with that kid and she ain't have it, he damn sure ain't leave nothing with Yandi's dumb ass, I know for a fact he wouldn't leave something like that with any of his niggas. He played off of my fears and got me for $40,000."

I was sitting there seething when Loon said, "Ain't that a good thing, though? I mean, yeah, you wasted a lot of time tryna find out who had the envelope, but now you know there ain't an envelope stopping you. Now you can hit the nigga whenever you want."

"You're absolutely right, Loon," I said, the fury I had boiling in my veins being quelled instantly. I called Shacago and didn't even wait for his greeting when he picked up. "Shacago, everything's been handled. We hitting that nigga, Quan, tonight."

CHAPTER 11

Hit 'Em Up

Shacago

*I*t was quiet when I arrived home. Xavier said Zarielle had spent the entire night waiting for me and should be asleep by now. When I saw all the lights were off, I was ready to do some praising until they clicked on and Zarielle stepped out of the kitchen with her arms crossed.

"Look who finally decided to show up," she said, taking in my disheveled appearance. "The same way you decided to show up on the morning of our wedding. You must think I'm stupid, Shacago. I know you fucked somebody else that night and I'm pretty sure it was the same bitch again."

"Zarielle, you tripping. I'm not fucking any—"

"Un-uh. You not coming up in here with that lying ass bullshit thinking it's gonna work again, Shacago. Is it Raven? She ain't look like your type, but what do I know at this point?"

"Zarielle—"

"Lemme guess, you and your baby momma decided to reunite for one last night of fucking and you decided to go back for more? No, that's not right. I was on Rosé's Instagram and she was at home last night being faithful to her man. You know who that leaves? That bitch you hired from Tasty. Admit it! You fucked her on our wedding night—"

"ZARIELLE, SHUT THE FUCK UP—"

"And you fucked her again," Zarielle continued like I hadn't even spoken. "Why won't you just be honest with me? She's beautiful. She's got that gorgeous skin you're always talking about. She's like a little Rosé without the baggage and that's what you like, isn't it? Somebody that reminds you of your better days. You don't have to lie to me, Shacago. I can see it in your eyes."

"Zarielle, I'm not about to stand here and do this with you," I told her as I made my way down the hall.

"I'm not asking you to do anything but tell me the truth! Tell me the truth, Shacago! Tell me the—"

"YES!" I roared, rounding on her. "Yes, I fucked her, but it ain't have nothing to do with no Rosé. I fucked her because I felt something, aight? Something I haven't felt with you in a long time. Normal. You're always worried about me being 'Shacago that runs shit' or 'Shacago the monster.' Have you ever loved 'Shacago the man'? That's what Rosé fell in love with and I feel the same thing happening with Parai, but I can't act on it. You know why? Because I'm stuck with you."

"Stuck with me?" Zarielle shrieked. "You think I wanna be with your bum ass? You think this was my first choice at happiness? Hell no! I could've done better than you a long ass time ago. My phone is full of men more than willing to give me everything I want without having to wait. Cars on demand, clothes on demand, and homes on demand. So how about I do you a favor and pack all my shit and leave this rinky dink apartment so you can enjoy your build-a-bitch in peace."

Zarielle pushed past me and made a beeline for our bedroom, slamming the door, and cussing up a storm behind it. I should've chased after her, but the morning I shared with Parai had me falling back. I had business to handle and I wasn't about to try and fix something that was probably broken beyond repair.

******

"You look like shit," Xavier said as he observed me over his shades.

"I slept on the couch all day today. Or should I say I *tried* sleeping on the couch today while Zarielle and her friends blasted *Lemonade* while packing her shit," I muttered, sinking into the passenger seat of the car and shutting my eyes.

"Packing her shit up for what?"

"We broke up."

"Broke up? Y'all ain't been married but for three weeks and two of them were spent on y'all honeymoon. What could have possibly happened for y'all to suddenly divorce?"

"I told her how I really feel. That, and I fucked somebody else."

"I knew it. So, the night of your bachelor party, you did fuck somebody. I bet it was that honey that you picked up from Tasty, wasn't it? She bad as fuck. I ain't even mad."

"Parai is more to me than just a fuck, aight? I see myself building something with her."

The car was silent for the rest of the ride. I had fallen into a deep sleep when Xavier shook me awake. We were parked in front of Rosé's building, and to be honest, all I wanted more than anything was some sleep. Xavier was still pensive in silence by the time we reached the front door.

"So, you plan on telling Rosé about your new girlfriend?" Xavier asked as he knocked on the door. "Or is she gon' find out when Zarielle shows up to the shop and tears it up?"

I didn't have to answer because the door opened and there stood Candice wearing a bright smile. "Hey, guys, good to see you. Where's Zarielle?"

"She couldn't make it, so X is taking her place," I said, refusing to give Rosé's nosy ass friend any ammunition.

If Candice noticed my snub, she didn't say anything and instead ushered us over to the living room. "Dinner is almost ready. Would you two like anything to drink?"

"Henny on the rocks," Xavier said, giving Candice his best bedroom eyes.

I sunk into the comfortable sofa and cosigned that with a hand raise. "I'll take the same."

With Candice gone, Xavier and I were left in another awkward silence. He was shaking his leg as his jaw worked. I thought it was strange behavior for my brother and decided to call him on it.

"Why do you care about Zarielle and I being together all of a sudden? You ain't like her from the beginning. I thought you'd be planning my divorce party by now, hitting up everybody for a night at the strip club after dinner."

"It's not that. I'm worried about Zarielle being a wildcard. Quan is her cousin and the last thing we need is her going back to him on some petty shit to get back at you."

"Zarielle is better than that."

Xavier shot me a look. "I take it that you ain't got much experience with scorned women. A bitch like Zarielle, with as much knowledge about everything we've been doing, is dangerous on the streets. She get to crying on her momma shoulder and then somebody gives her the bright idea to call the Feds. We all looking at life."

I hadn't thought about the consequences of our relationship ending on a bad note. That was one more problem that I had on my shoulders. However, it all disappeared when Rosé walked into the room holding a tumbler of Hennessey on the rocks with my name all over it. Xavier barely had his to his lips when mine was finished in three gulps. Rosé, being the perfect hostess, left and returned with the rest of the bottle.

"You look like you could use it," she said, pouring me another glass. "Here I was, thinking I was having a bad week."

"Why? 'Cause of that bullshit with Yandi?" Xavier asked while I sipped my drink at a slower pace this time around.

"That's exactly why. The nerve of her man to come and push up on me in my own house and then go back and tell her I wanted his corny ass. I hate the way this man has Yandi all turned out. I wish there was something I could do about it but everyone keeps saying that I need to let her…Xavier, why are you looking at me like that?"

Xavier was staring at Rosé like he'd struck gold. I looked from Rosé to my brother, unsure of what was about to happen next. Something told me that the grin spreading across Xavier's face was a prelude to a series of unfortunate events.

"What if I told you that I could help you with your Quan problem?"

Rosé eyed Xavier suspiciously. "What do I have to do?"

"All you gotta do is show up and be pretty."

******

"Xavier, are you sure about this? I'm not about to put my son's mother at risk behind this bullshit and something goes wrong…."

Xavier clapped my back and gave me a little shake. "Shacago, calm down. If Rosé plays this right, then we ain't got a damn thing to worry about. I promise this is gon' go real smooth."

"It better or else…" I said, wagging my finger at him as I opened the bedroom door and entered a suite made for a king.

Everything was white on white: the walls, the shag area rugs, the California king bed facing a white ceiling to floor entertainment center. Sitting at a white vanity wearing a rose gold teddy with a white silk robe was Rosé doing her makeup. I wasn't sure if it was the color scheme or the R&B music playing softly in the background, but I felt like I was intruding on a special moment.

"What?" Rosé asked with a hint of a smile as she studied me through the vanity mirror.

"Nothing...I was looking at you and it made me think about... forget it."

"No," Rosé said, cocking her head to the side. "I wanna know. You hate when people don't finish their thoughts, so I know you ain't about to do me like that."

"Aight, you got it," I said, holding my hands up in defeat. "I don't mean to make you uncomfortable or anything but...looking at you in here like this makes me think about how I used to picture how you would look on our wedding night."

Rosé's mouth flopped open and shut a few times before she settled with, "Wedding night? You pictured us getting married?"

"Of course I did. I was in love with you, Rosé, and I wanted to spend the rest of my life with you. A street nigga like me never thought about taking wedding vows until you. Honestly, I thought you were the only woman I would want that with. Sounds stupid, right?"

Rosé was staring at me through the mirror like she'd lost her best friend. Now it was my turn to ask her, "Why you looking at me like that?"

"Nothing, I was thinking about stuff."

"Speaking of stuff, you said you had something to tell me. What was it?"

Rosé stood up and hugged me tight. "I wanted to thank you for still being the wonderful man that I met all those years ago. I know I give you a lot of shit sometimes, but I'm proud of you, Shacago. For being an amazing father to our son and living up to your potential despite everything you've been through. I saw Parai's tattoo on Instagram and it's beautiful."

"I appreciate that, Rosé. After the day I've been through, I really needed to hear that."

"Y'all gon' have to cut this Kumbaya session short 'cause Quan just pulled up. He's parking and also by himself. Shacago, let's go."

Rosé headed downstairs to greet the guest of the night. Xavier and I split up, with me hiding in the bathroom shower while he took refuge inside of one of the large cabinets of the wall unit. We stilled when the bedroom door opened and Quan's awestruck voice filled the room.

"This shit is tight. I been to your spot, so whose is this?" Quan said, referring to the brownstone Xavier managed to get access to under a short amount of time.

"This is one of Marquise's weekend spots he recently purchased. He's out of town on business, so I figured I would make myself at home," Rosé lied nonchalantly. I could hear her pouring glasses of the Möet we picked up from the liquor store. "You can do the same. Take your shoes off and get comfortable."

"I ain't gon' even lie—this shit feels real sus. You wasn't feeling me the least bit the last time we saw each other and next thing I know, you inviting a nigga over for dinner? This ain't a setup, is it?" Quan asked jokingly.

"Of course, it is," Rosé replied. A second later she laughed. "I'm playing with you, Quan. Don't look at me like that."

"I can't help it. I love looking at you. Especially with what you got on right now."

"You weren't looking at me when we first met."

"I couldn't look at you like that with Yandi sitting next to me. You know how insecure she can be sometimes."

"You're right. Enough about Yandi, though. I invited you over to talk about us. First, let's toast to a surprise love connection," Rosé said, her voice silky and soft. I was standing here feeling real sorry for this nigga cause he was about to die with a hard on.

The clink of glasses was the first warning sign for us to get ready. Rosé was born with the ability to have any man undressed within a matter of minutes. I could picture her playing with her glass, taking tentative sips while Quan downed his after getting a good look at her in that teddy.

"You looking real good," Quan said after a minute. "Why don't you come over here and let a real nigga show you what you ain't been getting enough of."

"That's funny, because I can say the same. You been fucking around with these little ass girls and have no idea how a real woman gets down. Strip for me, papi," Rosé purred.

I heard Quan unbuckle his pants and the thud of his shoes hitting the hardwood floor. "What you about to do with those?" Quan asked, referring to the silk ties I gave Rosé earlier.

"Show you how I keep niggas crawling back to me. I didn't bag Marquise by lying on my back. Relax and let me take care of you," Rosé said sweetly and I already knew this nigga was silly putty in her hands.

The music in the bedroom grew louder, which was our second and final warning to get ready. I waited a full minute before slowly opening the bathroom door and sliding into the dimly lit room. Xavier opened the wall unit with ease, our eyes locking as he climbed out of it. Rosé was playing her part to the fullest as she kissed on Quan's neck while stroking his dick through the Calvin Klein briefs he wore. His wrists were tied to the headboard and I knew his eyes were crossed underneath the tie covering his them. Xavier and I crept to the head of the bed, laughing at the funny faces Rosé started making.

"Yo, when you gon' stop playing games and put ya mouth on it?" Quan asked, squirming as Rosé stroked his tip with a vengeful smile on her face.

Xavier stuck his gun in Quan's mouth and said, "Right after you get finished topping mines off.

Rosé ripped the tie off Quan's eyes. "Your cockiness was your downfall, bruh. If you would've humbled yourself and asked 'what would her fine ass want with a bitch nigga like me?' you could've saved yourself."

Quan tried to reply but Xavier shoved the gun deeper into his mouth until he started retching. Rosé, the queen of petty, kissed Quan on the forehead and stared at him squirming until she grew bored. I helped her shrug into her jacket and after chucking Xavier the deuces, we were off into the night.

"I cannot believe I actually helped the two of you handle 'business,'" Rosé said, using air quotes. "You promise I don't have to worry about this coming back to bite me in the ass?"

"We already got rid of the burner phone you used to text him with and trust me when I say ain't a single soul gon' find that nigga after X is done with him."

"Did he ever admit that it was Quan and them that jumped him?"

"Nah, but I'm assuming his pride was fucked up and he still ain't ready to tell the truth on that one. You know how Xavier can be…"

Rosé giggled. "Oh, do I. Xavier may be crazy, self-centered, and overdramatic, but he's got a good heart. His loyalty is rare."

"Which is why I'm grateful to have him on my team."

We spent the rest of the ride in a companionable silence, with Rosé staring out the window, humming the tune to the song on the radio. Nostalgia filled the car, reminding me of a time when Rosé and I would cruise around the city with a blunt, chilling and singing along to anything that played on the radio. Life was different now—we were parents and I was a married man. I was still reminiscing when I pulled up to her place.

"I'll see you bright and early at the shop?" Rosé said with a smile, looking like every part of the girl I met seven years ago.

"Of course. Make sure you get some sleep…"

Once Rosé was tucked inside of her home, I pulled off. I felt my phone vibrate and knew it was probably Xavier telling me that our business was handled. To my surprise, it was Parai.

Parai: *I've spent all day lying in bed waiting for this moment. Don't feel sorry for me because I had the time we shared this morning to keep me company. I know you can't promise me the world, Shacago, but I want to bring you into mine. I'm willing to do whatever it takes to make it work. Let's talk about it in the morning. XOXO.*

Staring at the message, I thought about the fight I had with Zarielle and the long day that followed it. For a second, Xavier's words had me second-guessing myself, thinking the threat Zarielle posed was enough for me to fall back in line and play it safe. Then I stared at these hugs and kisses sent just for me and decided risk was worth it.

Xavier

"Aahhhh," I mocked Quan as I pulled the gun out of his mouth. "You thought I was about to let you speak in front of Shacago and Rosé? Fuck outta here."

"You kill me you telling on yourself, or you forgot about that?" Quan asked coolly, eyeing me with a knowing look.

I let out a hearty chuckled and slapped that nigga with the butt of my gun. "I ain't telling on shit. I went and paid a visit to Nataysia and guess what I found out? Ain't no fucking envelope. Your bitch ass was just playing me for my chicken."

"Yo-you went and saw Nataysia?" Quan said, the cocky grin he always wore disappearing.

I gave him a cute little tap on the nose. "I killed the little bitch, too."

"You motherfu—"

"Yeah, I am fucking your mother. I'm also fucking up everything in your life right after I'm done with you. Nobody gets away with taking my money and running game on me. I told myself that when I got my hands on you, you would pay and I meant that shit."

"Caesar ain't gon' let you get away with this," Quan hissed before making a rumbling noise in his throat and chucking a glob of spit towards my face.

I caught it in my hand and slapped it on his face. "Caesar ain't letting me get away with this? Whose house you think we in right now?"

With two snaps of my fingers, the bedroom door opened and in walked my team along with some of México's finest. A black sack was thrown over Quan's head and he was led downstairs, where I would get to have my fun in Caesar's basement of horrors. This Brooklyn brownstone was beautiful—with five bedrooms, two living rooms, and a gourmet kitchen decorated with the best of the best—but the basement was where the real fun happened. Caesar was as sick as I was and admitted that he let Quan kill Deuce so he wouldn't have to get his hands dirty. His first option of who would take over the territory had always been me. And Shacago could help if he wanted.

Rogelio, Caesar's right hand, fell behind the group. I knew he was testing me, checking to make sure I could handle getting dirty, and I wasn't about to disappoint.

"What y'all got popping down there?" I asked, rubbing my hands together as I thought about all the fun I was about to have tonight.

"Lemme put it to you like this, we've had FBI agents break down there after just a little taste. You gon' have some fun, baby boy. You ready for this?"

I finally had everything I worked for: a higher position, more territory, and my money was about double. There was only one obvious answer.

"Nigga, of course I'm ready. I was born for this. Them necks I stepped on wasn't for nothing."

One Week Later...

Peace.

Quiet.

Silence.

"Daddy, it's so good to spend time with you at your place," Gabi said, lowering the stem of grapes to my waiting lips. "This is the quality time I've been missing. What's going on with your girlfriend?"

I bit off two grapes and chewed them while I mulled over my response. I settled with, "Man, fuck that bitch. She still over there at her momma's house having a temper tantrum, but she already know that when I'm ready for her to return to Shacago then she will."

"I could've sworn I saw Shacago all over IG with some other chick. She's bad as fuck, too. I don't know if he's gonna leave all that for Zarielle," Gabi stated matter-of-factly.

"That bitch gon' do whatever Shacago say and if that means going back to being a side chick, she'll do it without a problem. Ain't no need to worry about—"

My phone rang for the tenth time in the past three hours. Who was it calling once again?

"Good morning, Yandi. How may I help you?" I said in my best uppity voice.

A whole bunch of ugly crying filled my earpiece followed by Yandi screaming, "I know you had something to do with him disappearing, motherfucker!!"

"Yandi, what are you over there crying and screaming about?"

I asked, plucking two more grapes into my mouth. "Talk to ya baby daddy about it."

"Quan has been missing for a week! Nobody from his team has seen him and he's not answering anyone's phone calls! Don't play stupid with me, Xavier! I've been doing some asking around and nobody saw you the last night he was seen."

Gabi politely took the phone from me and said, "That's because he was all up in my pussy last weekend, bitch!" She handed it back at once, Yandi's screams filling the quiet bedroom. "Sorry, daddy, but you know I always gotta look out for you."

I had Gabi's face halfway to mine when Yandi's voice came through loud and clear.

"WE'LL SEE HOW FUNNY IT IS WHEN I GIVE SHACAGO THIS ENVELOPE!"

My blood froze. "Wh-what the fuck are you talking about?"

"Oh, so now I have your attention! I woke up this morning and found an envelope with a note sitting on my doorstep. It said that in the event that Quan went missing for longer than seven days, this envelope was to be dropped off to me. Well it has Shacago's name on it, so I'm guessing it might have something to do with all the grimy shit I hear you do behind his back."

"Yandi, you better not give Shacago—"

"I'll do whatever I damn well please, nigga. And if I'm lucky, your ass will disappear just like Quan."

The click of the phone was a slap in the face. I wasn't sure how long I sat there until Gabi gave me a gentle shake and asked me what was wrong. I jumped out of bed, tripping and stumbling into my pants as I ran down the hall. Gabi followed me down the hall, her hands on her hips as she watched me stumble around the living room knocking stuff over until I found my favorite Glock.

"If anybody asks—"

"You been here with me all day," Gabi finished as she held the door open for me. "Be safe, daddy. Don't do nothing I wouldn't do."

Knowing Gabi, that ain't take nothing off the list—it added some more.

******

"X, maybe she was bluffing," Loon said as we sat parked at the end of the block, watching Shacago's shop for any sign of Yandi. "All she ever do is talk shit, anyways."

"That wouldn't explain how she knew about the envelope and Quan's specific directions. I checked Yandi, that little girl, and we chased all his niggas out the neighborhood. There ain't nobody else that could've known about this. We followed that nigga everywhere. I asked him time and time again after I water boarded his ass and he admitted that he lied."

"Of course he said he lied; you was gon' kill him anyway. He died and left you with a larger problem—what to do about your baby mother."

I sat up in my seat when I saw Yandi hop out of an Uber. She was all dressed up in a white pantsuit with some gold Giuseppes on her feet. She surveyed the driver of the car over her gold Gucci shades and winked, watching the car drive off before making her way towards the shop.

"Pull up on her," I ordered Loon as I shot God a silent prayer for forgiveness. "We gotta make this shit quick."

I loved my son with all my heart. He was my world and there wasn't a damn thing I wouldn't do for him. Lie. Cheat. Steal. So long as it guaranteed him a better life than I had without my pops, the Little X would have whatever his heart desired. My father treated us like shit and left my mother with two mouths to feed. I'll be damned if I ever left him to be raised by the streets.

Even if it meant killing his mother.

"Surprise, you stupid bitch!"

Yandi turned around and to my delight, the last thing she saw before checking out was the kiss I blew her. My hittas rolled up behind us, AKs out as they lit up every storefront along the quiet street. Over the hail of bullets was the sound of raining glass, spraying the sidewalks like a sharp thunderstorm. Yandi's feet remained rooted to the ground as her body danced with the bullets that tore through it, the exploding glass of Shacago's storefront windows made it look like a Harlem Shake revival. When the bullets stopped, Yandi (or what was left of her) spun slowly and hit the ground with a resounding thud. I pulled off and let my hittas handle the dirty business of taking that envelope off her person.

"Man, that shit was crazy," Loon said as he turned onto a backstreet and to take us to the chop shop where a brand-new car awaited us.

"Who you telling," I replied, shrugging out of my hoodie and beginning to strip off everything that would be dumped right along with the car. "I ain't wanna take my baby moms out, but the stupid bitch was asking for it. You see how she showed up to Shacago's shop? In a pimp suit with the 'I'm about to ruin your life' 11s on."

My burner phone lit up with a phone call from a foreign number. It rang twice and stopped, letting me know that the envelope had been taken from Yandi and our business was handled. Loon turned on the radio, filling the radio with Drake's "Fake Love."

"Nigga, what you got planned for tonight?"

"I don't know about you, but I got a bad bitch and a blunt waiting for me at home."

CHAPTER 12

Fallen Angel

Shacago

$\mathcal{R}$osé and I stood slowly, staring at the door riddled with bullet holes and then at each other. We stood there in silence until the sounds of squealing tires sounded through the shop. I opened the door with little effort—the knob had been blown off—and stepped into the rest of the shop.

Or what used to be shop.

I had a clear view of the street from where my windows used to be. Shards of glass littered the floor, crunching with every step I took. The cabinets had been torn apart by the assault of bullets and I could only imagine what my hand painted artwork looked like. A movement from my left shoved me back to reality and I was reminded that Rosé and I weren't the only ones in the shop.

"What the fuck was that?" Suede asked as I helped him shake the glass off his clothes.

Rosé disappeared into Raven's station and helped her out as well. Kidd, who had been taking a nap in my studio, appeared and propped himself up against the wall as he stared openmouthed at the sight. We all met in the hallway, and after five minutes of shock, the boys held the girls, who had started crying. *What if Parai hadn't texted me that she would be late?* I thought as I made my way to the front of the store. *She would be dead right now.* Just the thought of losing—

"No!" I screamed as I grew closer and got a look at the body on the floor outside the shop.

My legs gave out as I reached her, the pinches from the glass cutting my hands going unnoticed as I turned the body over. I brushed her hair away from her face and nearly threw up my breakfast. Everyone started filing outside, but I stopped them with a wave of my hand. My neighbors had already started trickling out of their shops, the crunching of glass echoing down the street.

"All of y'all get back inside!" I shouted, hoping Rosé would follow directions for once.

"It ain't Parai, is it?" Suede asked, covering the doorway so no one could get past.

I shook my head. "Nah, it ain't her. Now, please make sure you keep Rosé inside."

"Why do I need to be kept inside?" I heard Rosé ask from behind Suede.

"Rosé," I said, my throat growing thick as I took another look at Yandi's body. "For once in your life, do what I say!"

"Rosé, chill," Suede said as Rosé tried to push past him. "Stop tryna get around me and stay inside like Shacago—shit!"

Rosé stopped fighting with Suede and climbed out of the window. She stood rooted to the spot for what felt like ages when an unhuman wail escaped her lips. I had been holding it together until Rosé plopped down and pulled Yandi onto her lap, brushing her hair away from her face as she murmured apologies.

"I'm sorry, Yandi," she sobbed, rocking Yandi's bullet-ridden body back and forth. "I tried to save you, but I couldn't. Oh my God, I'm sorry. I don't know who did this, but you didn't deserve it…"

Taking in Rosé holding the dead body of her cousin, my destroyed shop, and the faces of all the other small business owners on the block, I knew I was out of my element. All of these innocent people became victims the moment I built this shop. This devastation could've been prevented had I not thought I was more than Shacago, a street nigga. I hung my head, sickened at what I caused, and made a decision I would never forget or regret.

Rosé's Tattoo Shop was closed for good.

******

"Shacago, you can't let one incident ruin the shop for you. You poured your heart and soul into that shop—"

"And had to watch an ambulance scrape someone off the ground because of me. Was Yandi perfect? Of course not—none of us are. But she ain't deserve to go out the way she did—behind some beef that X and I had with her nigga. I'm positive his people came back and did this for revenge."

"Revenge? Shacago, what did you go out there and do?" Parai

asked, scooting closer to me and taking my hand into hers.

"It doesn't matter what I did—it's done. I gotta worry about being there for my nephew when we tell him his mother ain't coming home." I placed my head in Parai's lap, relaxing when she began to rub her hands through my hair.

Parai drew small circles into my back with her nail, the sensation sending chills down my spine. "Well you don't need to worry about that tonight. How about I draw you a bath and I run to your place to pick you up some clothes?"

"Parai, I can't ask you to do that…"

"You didn't ask—I offered. Let me take care of you, baby." Parai made a move to get up, but I wouldn't let her. "Shacago—"

"All that other shit can wait. I don't need a meal, a bath, or even sleep. I need you. This morning, I thought that was you lying in front of the shop and nearly lost my mind. Knowing you're right here, safe in my arms, is everything I need right now. I know we ain't been together but a week, but…I think I'm falling in love with you."

"Falling? Shacago, I've loved you since the day we met. I guess I was trying to push you on Rosé because if it wasn't me, then she would be the one you're supposed to be with. It's been my goal to see you happy and seeing you like this is killing me. Please, let me take care of you."

I had been in my fair share of relationships—I had a life long before Rosé and Zarielle—but never had any woman I'd been with taking care of me. My entire life has been nothing but me being strong for everyone when I've wanted to do nothing more than succumb. Parai, with her gentle touch and warm words of encouragement, was breaking down walls I wasn't even aware that I had up. I closed my eyes and did something I hadn't been able to do in a long time.

Let go and blindly trust.

Xavier

"Hey, stranger," I said to Zarielle as she entered the bedroom she once shared with my brother. "Looking for Shacago, weren't you?"

Zarielle's eyes darted around the room, focusing on everything except me. "I got a text from his phone saying to meet him here, so I—"

"Finally came back to fix your fuck up before I found out? Yeah, I know all about you getting into some petty ass argument with him last week and not bothering to tell me about it. We're supposed to be a team, Zarielle! This ain't no fly-by-night shit we got going on! Why is it that I had to hear about you and my brother breaking up from him?"

"Because I knew you would react like this!" Zarielle shouted, kicking the door in frustration. "I do everything you ask me to, Xavier, and you're never grateful. Run some drugs to another state? Done. Fuck this nigga so we can get a better arms deal? Done. Fuck your brother and become his girlfriend. Done and done. But what I can't do is allow any man to blatantly disrespect me especially after taking me to another country and marrying me!"

"That's what you mad about? We almost got caught fucking in the kitchen and you sitting here mad about this nigga getting some ass on the side?" I let out a bark of laughter so loud Zarielle bumped into the threshold. "You stupid bitch, your loyalty ain't to Shacago—it's to me! Who gives a fuck about what he's out there fucking because at the end of the day that ain't securing our future! That's not paying the bills, and it damn sure ain't buying you that engagement ring you been eyeing for the past month. You think I ain't notice? Of course I did, Zarielle, because I notice everything."

"Then you must have noticed how miserable I've been and not given a fuck. I'm the mother of your child, Xavier, and I'm starting to feel like you don't give a fuck about neither one of us," Zarielle sobbed, tears pouring down her cheeks.

I ain't even have to check my watch to know that this argument had gone on for too long. The point of bringing Zarielle here wasn't to argue—I needed her back in Shacago's good graces now, while grief would allow it.

"Z, everything I'm doing right now is for us. You need to see the bigger picture. If Shacago is fucking that girl and they end up falling in love, guess what happens? You get alimony, child support, and half of anything he puts in his name so long as you ask. We wait a while, maybe like a year or two, and get together on some surprise shit. Shacago will be so happy and in love that he won't even care. Do you know how much it killed me to watch y'all get married in DR? That cut me deep, but I didn't walk around bitching over it because why? I respect what you're doing for us and I see the bigger picture."

Zarielle wiped her eyes. "Xavier, do you love me?"

Did I love Zarielle? Nah, probably not, but it wasn't something to take personal. I don't love nobody but my son and moms. However, I knew the fitting words for this moment was, "Of course I do. Now come and give your man a hug."

Zarielle and I had barely connected when we heard it.

"Was that—"

"The door closing? Yeah, I'll be right back," I said, brushing past her and running down the hall.

Whoever was there tried their best to shut the door quietly. Too bad they fucked up from the beginning and was about to get a piece of my mind. Or my piece. I snatched the door open and there stood Shacago's new girlfriend, her eyes wide with shock.

"Look at who we have here?" I leaned in the doorway. "You find everything you was looking for?"

Shacago's weekend bag was clutched tightly in her trembling hand. She must've ducked into the hallway closet when she heard me enter the house. "Ye-yeah, I was here to pick up some stuff for Shacago."

"So then why didn't you come and say hello instead of hiding in the closet?"

"I didn't—"

"'Cause you was looking to hear about some shit that ain't none of your business, that's why. Don't stand here and play that innocent act that everyone else eats up, my brother included. That's how you got him to stop fucking with my girl, right?"

"I don't know what you're talking—"

"Oh, you *do* know what I'm talking about because you stood in the closet listening to it. You know all about me and Zarielle being together, our child, how we been playing Shacago all this time like a fool."

Gone was the innocence replaced by Parai's cold glare. "You're not even ashamed of it. Shacago's been nothing but good to both of you and you're playing him for what? A game he doesn't want?"

"That's exactly why I'm playing him. Before he got locked up, my brother had it all. Money. Cars. Power. He should've walked out of jail like a king. You know what he came back as? A broke, snitching ass has-been. I know he flipped on Gabriel and lived with the guilt of it. Who you think told Gabriel about it? My loyalty for my brother died a long time ago and I told myself that I would bring fear back into the Stanfield name."

"You haven't brought anything but disgrace," Parai sneered, turning her nose up at me like some little Rosé wannabe. "Ain't nobody scared of you."

I let out a boisterous laugh. "You should be. You thought I was gon' tell you all of that and let you live? Come here, you stupid bitch!"

My hand clamped around Parai's wrist at the same time she swung the bag at my face, knocking me back into the apartment. The bitch was fast—she was halfway to the stairs when I grabbed her by the hair and yanked her into my arms, squeezing her chest so tight that she could barely breathe.

"You bitches keep thinking this is a game for me. This is my life y'all keep tryna fuck with. Do me a favor, though. When you get to hell, tell my baby mother to keep her head game strong. When I see her there, I want a warm welcome."

Rosé

"I still can't believe she's gone," I told Elijah and Tracey for the umpteenth time. "One minute we're fighting and the next—"

"Honey, you can't continue to beat yourself up like this," Tracey said as she took me into her arms. She rocked me back and forth like the mother I was missing. "You did everything you could for Yandi. No matter what happened yesterday, she knew you loved her and she would want you to stay strong for Little X."

After hearing the news of his mother's death, Little X had become a recluse, hiding in Cago's old room and refusing to speak with anyone. This would've been the perfect time for Xavier to step up to the plate and take care of him, but in usual Xavier fashion, he was nowhere to be found. *He's probably drowning in grief,* I thought as I snuggled into Tracey's arms. *I sure know I am.*

"You're the last person that should feel any guilt; you tried to make us get help for Yandi but everyone was all into their own issues…"

We lapsed into a comfortable silence when Elijah's phone rang. His entire demeanor changed immediately. He jumped out of his seat and was at the door before Tracey or I could react.

"Elijah, where are you going?" I yelled, rushing out into the early morning cold right behind him.

"Rosé, I have some business to handle."

I climbed into the back seat and buckled myself in before he could object. We were mourning the loss of family and here he was, running off to work. *Two can play this game*, I thought as I crossed my legs and waited for him to pull off.

"Rosé—"

"Eli, drive. There isn't anything you can say to make me get out of this car. Your family needs you, *I* need you. We're going to go wherever you're going together and coming right back."

Elijah pulled out without further argument, his hands gripping the steering wheel so tight his veins were popping out. We spent the rest of the ride in a tense silence, with me texting Shacago while Eli sat rigid as a board. It wasn't until we arrived at the scene, a local playground, did I understand why he was so uptight.

"Eli, what happened?" I asked, my face pressed against the window as I watched the dozen or so FBI agents working the scene, some standing in small clusters while others were on the outskirts talking on the phone.

"Someone called in and reported a body this morning," Elijah replied, taking a calming breath. "Usually we don't respond to homicides, but it was an informant for the FBI. Let's hope there's enough for us to make a positive ID. Here, put on my windbreaker so no one will notice you."

Numb to the idea of seeing two bodies in two days, I followed Elijah through the crowd of agents to where the body was. We were almost there when Elijah stopped suddenly. I bumped into his back, nearly hitting the floor if not for the help of the agent behind me.

"Elijah, what's—oh my God! Parai!"

Tossed in the bushes like some unwanted garbage was Parai. Her hair was pulled away from her face, revealing choke marks around her neck. The dress she wore was ripped to shreds. None of this was what made me recognize her—it was the tattoo on her thigh, a raw and naked self-portrait that I recognized instantly. Shacago. How was I going to tell Shacago about this? The question was still racing through my mind when I turned around and stared up at Elijah, who was rigid.

"Eli, what's wrong?" I said, shaking him.

Elijah turned away from Parai's body, his jaw working overtime before he replied, "I...uh...they called me down here for an informant. I had no idea it would be my own."

I knew my brother well enough to know that he wasn't being completely honest with me. Then I thought about the cookout where I thought he was spying on Shacago, who was talking to Parai. I also remembered the other night when he came in disheveled. *I have to strip whenever I meet my informant...*

"You were fucking her," I said, backing away from Elijah when he refused to look at me. "You've been fucking her the whole time, haven't you? Haven't you?"

Elijah finally looked at me, except now his eyes were pleading for me to be quiet. "Rosé, we can talk about this later! Right now, I'm at wor—"

"I don't give a damn where we are. You were fucking your informant, and now she's dead. Do you know what that looks like?"

Elijah opened his mouth to reply when someone else replied, "A motive for murder."

Sean Corbett, the Special Agent in Charge also Elijah's boss, approached us with two agents flanking him. I recognized them from family gatherings and knew there was a good chance they wouldn't be invited to any after this. I was mad at Elijah, but not enough to sell him out to his job.

"That's not what I was about to say—"

"It doesn't matter what you were about to say. What matters is that due to some findings, we're placing you under arrest, Agent Hughes, for the murder of Parai Santigual."

I watched as my brother, who had given the Bureau all his time, energy, and youth, was handcuffed and led to an unmarked car like a common criminal. Glancing back at Parai's body, it broke my heart to know that I would have to bring more bad news to the team than we already needed. If the destruction of his shop wasn't enough, the news of Parai's death was likely to take Shacago over the edge.

******

I found him standing in the middle of the mess, staring at what was once his pride and joy, that was now nothing more than rubble and dust. The hood was ruthless—people had already come in and stolen the pictures off the walls. I wouldn't be the least bit surprised if they stole our equipment, too. Shacago turned abruptly, his eyes momentarily lit up until he saw it was me. I knew that look and this became even harder for me.

"Don't look too excited," I joked, approaching him slowly, the crushed glass beneath my sneakers making me cringe.

Shacago ran a hand over his head. "I ain't mean to play you like that, Rosé. I was looking for someone else."

"Parai?" I said, playing with my fingers to keep him from noticing how bad my hands were shaking.

"Yeah, last night I fell asleep at her place and when I woke up she wasn't there. I checked my apartment, asked my neighbors if they had seen her. Nobody's heard anything."

His first sentence caught me off guard. "Her place?"

"I know this isn't the best time to tell you this, with everything you been through yesterday, but Parai and I are together. It ain't been long—only a week—but I'm telling you, she's the one."

"Shacago—"

"I know what you're about to say, and yes: Zarielle and I are still married. I'm gonna handle my business and make sure I set her up real good for everything I put her through."

I felt like I was going to be sick. "Sh-Shacago—"

"Rosé, just hear me out. I know we're supposed to run stuff like this by each other before everyone knows, but I didn't want to jinx it. She's the one. I know everyone will say it's too soon and that we barely know each other. None of that matters to me; Parai matters to me. She reminds me of what you and I used to have. I love her. Rosé, what's wrong with you?"

Sometime during Shacago's speech, I had covered my ears and began shaking my head back and forth as I cried. I couldn't listen to any of this. I couldn't bear to tell this man that the woman he loved was dead.

"Shacago…there's something I have to tell you." I swiped at my eyes, praying for the tears to stop. "Parai…Parai was found dead this morning. Somebody strangled her to death."

Shacago cracked a smile. "That's not true, Rosé. She was just with me last night. She went to grab some clothes from my place and…I haven't heard from her since."

Soon I wasn't the only one crying. Shacago placed his head on my shoulder and cried with me, the only thing heard throughout the shop. We were both broken by death and like him, I knew I could never step another foot in this shop. We tried, failed, and maybe in the future we would try again, but one thing was for sure.

Rosé's Tattoo Shop was over.

CHAPTER 13

A Flaw in The Plan

$\mathcal{S}$he entered the hospital room with a smile, watching as her little sister read the book she purchased her at the gift shop. Nataysia tore her eyes from the book and greeted her with the same smile they had inherited from their father.

"I've been waiting for you to stop by all day. Where've you been?" Nataysia asked, tossing the book aside and giving her, her undivided attention.

She pulled up the seat she had slept in from the night she found Nataysia in the hospital, fresh out of surgery. The doctors told her that it was nothing short of a miracle that the bullet meant for Nataysia's forehead managed to graze her scalp, causing a long gash across the top of her head where the bullet split her wig in two. That same wig is what cushioned her fall when she kicked her chair over. One of her little home girls trying to sneak in a quickie with her boyfriend found her, proving that miracles happen more often than she thought. If Nataysia would have died—

"Kem?" Nataysia said to her big sister, who had spaced out once again like she had been ever since she got out of jail last week. "Where were you?"

Kem fingered the envelope in her jacket pocket. It was the last thing her boyfriend, Quan, had left behind to take care of her and her family. "I was out securing our future."

TO BE CONTINUED

CONNECT WITH TYA MARIE

Facebook: https://www.facebook.com/AuthoressTyaMarie

For exclusive sneak peeks join my **Readers Group: Tea with Tya Marie** https://www.facebook.com/groups/318594828537945/

Instagram: Tya_Marie1028

Twitter: LaTya_Marie

Looking for a publishing home?

Royalty Publishing House, Where the Royals reside, is accepting submissions for writers in the urban fiction genre. If you're interested, submit the first 3-4 chapters with your synopsis to submissions@royaltypublishinghouse.com.

Check out our website for more information: www.royaltypublishinghouse.com.

Text ROYALTY to 42828 to join our mailing list!

To submit a manuscript for our review, email us at submissions@royaltypublishinghouse.com

Text RPHCHRISTIAN to 22828 for our CHRISTIAN ROMANCE novels!

Text RPHROMANCE to 22828 for our INTERRACIAL ROMANCE novels!

Get LiT!

Download the LiT eReader app today and enjoy exclusive

content, free books, and more

Do You Like CELEBRITY GOSSIP?

Check Out QUEEN DYNASTY!
Visit Our Site: www.thequeendynasty.com

CPSIA information can be obtained
at www.ICGtesting.com
Printed in the USA
LVOW10s2026270417
532438LV00014B/361/P